Bloodline of the Nile

Emma Sheridan

Contents

Prologue

Centuries The gods once walked the Earth, and they bestowed some of their powers on mortals.

But there was one god who stood out from the rest.

Her name was BASTET.

Her beauty was greater than the seven wonders of the world, her power was the envy of the other gods, and her fury was that of a lioness.

She was the goddess of life and protection.

She bestowed her power on the mortals, making them the first generation of the Lynx.

The Lynx were extremely powerful cat shifters.

"Eyes / Daughter of Ra" was also the goddess of the sun and the moon.

Bastet was destined to bring peace and unity to the world.

bringing gods and mortals together and ushering in a new age of gods.

Set was a more sinister deity who desired power and wanted to sit on the throne as Ra's Successors.

He would also bestowed his power on his worshipers, who were jackal shifters.

Set was successful in killing Bastet.

Ra wept for his daughter and bestowed upon her nine lives to live, grow, love, cry, and fulfill her great destiny.

Incarnating as Maya.

Seth will have to do everything in his power to prevent Maya from fulfilling her destiny.

Maya is now in the midst of a war and must prevent the jackals and lynx from killing each other.

Give new life to her people, unite the world, and claim the throne that was destined for her.

All in Bastet.

Chapter 1

The Night did not always belong to vampires and werewolves; it once belonged to the Lynx and the Sha.

Majestic creatures that ruled the night and shielded Egypt from numerous threats.

There were many different gods with varying powers long ago when they shared the Earth with mortals.

However, the Egyptian pantheon of gods was more ancient, as they possessed the ability to transform into animals. Some of these gods were half human, half beast.

They were primal and fearsome.

People who worshiped these gods were endowed with their abilities.

Bastet, however, was more powerful than the rest.

Ra was a titan, the sun, and the uncle of Zeus, the lightning god. She was Ra's heir and successor, the most powerful being in the universe.

He ruled over the Egyptian pantheon of gods.

He was aware that, after battling Apophis for a millennium to prevent Egypt and the entire universe from being devoured, he would eventually pass away and rest.

There were a lot of gods because as the population of mortals increased, their desire, resentment, and suffering would give rise to new deities.

Seth, also referred to as Set, was one of them.

He was a Sha, a creature that looked like a cross between a jackal, a hyena, and a dog.

Bastet bestowed her power on mortals, and they became the Lynx, powerful cat shifters with great powers.

She was going to be her father's heir, take his power and throne, and finally defeat Apophis the Great Darkness, but Set was not going to let that happen.

He had other plans and wanted to use Apophis to rule the Earth and all the gods.

He plotted, and with the assistance of his worshipers, whom he had blessed with his power, they were able to attack Bast's temple, killing her a day before her coronation, before she inherited her father's powers and became primordial.

With the last of his power, Ra blessed his daughter with nine lives.

Nine lives to live, fall in love, make mistakes, find herself, but most importantly, fulfill her destiny.

He also cursed Set and his children, making them the lowest of all shifters and rendering them almost powerless.

Now reduced to nothing more than a Sha shifter, Set no longer a god he turned into stone and was carried by his people for hundreds of years.

Ra passed away, leaving the throne vacant.

His throne radiated power, and anyone attempting to ascend to the throne would meet their demise. Only his heir would hold the position.

Now that both Bastet and her father had vanished, the remaining gods decided to end their human existence and go back to their own world to battle Apophis in order to prevent him from consuming Ra's creation, which was being led by Sobek.

Seth and his people were soon met with resistance from the Lynx, who fought back, and a war ensued.

Sha against Lynx.

For centuries, they have been killing each other.

The lynx waited for Bastet to be reborn and return to claim her throne and aid them in defeating the evil Sha, but she never appeared.

Bastet's story has been passed down from generation to generation.

Most people began to believe it was a myth.

But it was not because she was finally reborn.

And now the war can finally begin.

Chapter 2

"M aya "

"Maya," she heard her name called, but she did not care.

She looked out the window at the city where she grew up.

The metropolis of Metro City.

"Yes!" She finally responded when her mother's assistant called.

Returning to her mind and looking around, she realized where she was.

Another day another photoshoot for her.

The most famous supermodel in the world.

One of the most recognizable faces in the world was hers.

She was the face of many companies and her image was seen all over the world.

She possessed the beauty and demeanor of ancient royalty, at least that was how they characterized her.

She felt like the world was hers.

She had everything, and her beauty was unparalleled.

Aside from conversing with her mom,

"Not right now, she is on the phone with Shanghai," the assistant explained as she refused to do anything else until her mother arrived.

" Honey, what exactly is it?" Sophie asked her daughter.

"I have been feeling strange, and I am not sure I can do this anymore."

"I feel like I am sick of this life." Maya informs her stunned mother.

"After we get your hundredth vogue cover and the biggest photographer is here, not to mention Anna Wintour is on her way, this is when you decide." Sophie says this to Maya as her assistant hands her the phone.

"A call from Australia," the assistant murmured.

" Get ready, because we are going to talk about your internal crisis. Do not embarrass me today." Sophie informs Maya.

" But Mom you always say we will talk and then you never have time for me.

"I am on every billboard in this city, every bench, every bus, and every magazine, but it is as if you do not see me." Maya informs her mother, who was already on the phone.

" Just get ready," Sophie says to her daughter as she lowers her phone.

Maya could not believe it as she made her decision as well.

She bolted from the room, running away from everything.

When they saw her leave, her mother abruptly terminated the call.

Maya dashed out of the exit and onto the street, where people began to stare at her and recognize her, taking pictures and invading her space.

" Maya, Maya, Maya " they screamed. Maya could not think because she was too confused, but she felt her handheld as she looked and saw it was Ivan as he saved her from the crowd and they got into his car, and he immediately sped away.

Sophie was disappointed and enraged as she looked out the window of the studio building.

" I thought I was coming to see you at your photoshoot, " Ivan asked.

"It was fun at first, but now it is sucking the life out of me, and my mom can not look at me for more than two seconds." "I could not stand it another minute." Maya confides in her boyfriend.

" Your mother is going to be furious!" Ivan tells her.

"I skipped on her and Anna Wintor and I was on the streets of Metro City in sweats and probably all those pictures are on the internet and I do not care," Maya says as they both laugh.

" You are very brave for standing up for yourself and your voice. "You have done everything your mother has asked of you since I can remember, and perhaps it is time to do what you ask of yourself." Ivan tells her, and she finds it hard to believe.

"Baby, you are truly unique." She says, glancing at him after he dropped her off at her house.

"Do not be depressed and give me a call if you need anything." he said to her as she exited his car and watched him drive away,

she was greeted by the concierge.

As she ascended the elevator and arrived on the floor, she went to her bedroom and jumped onto her bed, where she promptly fell asleep.

"You are your father's daughter," her father told her as they played in the ruins of an ancient Egyptian temple.

"What is that? " She inquired of her father because there was a drawing on the wall.

Connor smiled as he drew the small chain with the same sign from around his neck.

"This is the insignia of the goddess Bastet; she was the most beautiful woman in the world, and her beauty was matched by her intelligence and fighting spirit.

She knew who she was.

She is everything that I see in you." He said to her as she hugged him and waking up from the dream she began packing up her clothes she looked at her bedstand and picked up a frame with a picture of her and her father with the pyramids behind them.

She also packed the picture before telling Ivan.

She looked around her room, took her suitcase, and left, leaving a note for her mother on her bed.

Arriving at the airport, Ivan and her friends were already there.

"What are all of you doing here?" She asked.

" Going to Egypt with you," Lucia says as Maya sighs and embraces her best friend.

"Ash, you are coming too," Maya exclaimed, hugging him.

" Anything for you, beautiful, we would go to the end of the world with you." He said as they hugged.

" I had nothing important to do, so I am coming." Emmy broke up the happy reunion.

"I am happy you came," Maya says to her.

"When I saw the video, I thought you might need us," Emmy explained.

" She was the one who suggested we accompany you to Egypt. " Ivan added as Maya smiled seeing all her friends as her head began pounding she almost lost her balance but Ivan held her.

" Are you okay? " He asked.

"Just the headaches and exhaustion have been crushing me." Maya says as she felt something and looked around and looked to the entrance of the airport and saw her mother and her body-guards arrive.

"Allow me to speak with her," she says.

"We are here for you." Lucia commented.

Maya went to talk to her mother, and they sat down.

"You are leaving, and all I get is a note?" She asks her daughter.

"Yes, because that is how we seem to communicate these days, I am leaving, and you will not stop me." Maya tells her mother.

"I am not here to stop you; I just want to know if this is what you want because your father left us for a reason," she says to Maya who understood her parents differences.

"I know you are worried about me traveling alone, but I will be fine, and my friends are coming." Maya reassures her.

"You can not just walk away every time you do not like something. We signed contracts, and you have obligations to my model agency." Sophie tells Maya.

"It's funny how you throw that word around when all my life I have given you exactly that.

I wanted to make you happy, so I gave up my childhood.

I missed prom, my graduation, my friends' birthdays, and getting out with my friends. I also missed being normal to make you happy.

I was working on commercials and photo shoots on the set.

I am grateful for the life you have given me, but when I look in the mirror, I see nothing.

Beyond everything you have transformed me into, I have no idea who I am. With a tear streaming down her cheek, Maya tells her mother.

Is that the reason you are traveling to Egypt in search of your father? Sophie asks her daughter.

"I am not fleeing; rather, I am fleeing to something else. I have always been yours, so now please allow me to go find my identity. Perhaps if I get to know my father, I will be able to better understand who I am.

I am so grateful to you for being the parent who never left, and for always stepping up to take care of me. I love you.

This doesn't mean I don't love you any less," Maya explained.

"He is your father, and I can never change that," Sophie says to her daughter as Maya stands up and kisses her mother on the cheek.

"When did I raise such a beautiful, brave, and wise daughter full of wisdom and compassion?" Sophie said this while touching Maya's face.

"Do not worry, I will put him through the grill," Maya assures her mother as she heads back to her boyfriend and friends. Sophie watches as they left to go board the plane.

Going further and further into the airport.

Maya was dead set on finding the thing that would give her life meaning and discovering why her father had abandoned her.

Sophie returned to her limo and pulled out her phone.

"She is coming to Cairo and I expect not a single hair on my girl is touched or you will make an enemy of me," she said hugging up the phone.

Maya awoke on the plane that night with more pain coursing through her body, and when she looked next to her seat, her boyfriend was already asleep.

Getting up she saw almost everyone was asleep as she went to the bathroom to wash her face.

Inhaling and exhaling.

Looking in the mirror and noticing her eyes are a different color.

"What am I becoming?" Maya muttered as all she saw in the mirror was a reflection of herself.

It was her face, but the person looking back was fierce and powerful.

Maya had no idea who she was, and hoped her father would tell her so she would know what to do next.

Chapter 3

"Maya wake up and look," Ivan whispered as she woke up to the warm sun on her face and looking out of the plane's window to see the pyramids.

"Home," she said with a smile on her face looking out the window as it was a new day.

"Welcome home Maya ," Ivan whispered as Maya was gleaming with joy.

Getting off the plane Maya hid herself with a disguise not to get unwanted attention for herself and her friends.

"Egypt has one of the longest histories of any country, tracing its heritage along the Nile Delta back to the 6th-4th millennia BCE.

Considered a cradle of civilisation," Lucia explained as they took their luggage from customs.

"Ancient Egypt saw some of the earliest developments of writing, agriculture, urbanisation, organised religion and Iconic monuments such as the Giza Necropolis and its Great Sphinx, as well the ruins of Memphis, Thebes, Karnak, and the Valley of the Kings, reflect this legacy and remain a significant focus of scientific and popular interest.

Egypt's long and rich cultural heritage is an integral part of its national identity.

Egypt was an early and important centre of Christianity, but was largely Islamised in the seventh century and remains a predominantly Sunni Muslim country, albeit with a significant Christian minority, along with other lesser practiced faiths." Lucia explained to the group as they had left the taxi and were waiting for their car when Lucia stopped and her jaw dropped.

It was a giant billboard of Maya with the caption of welcome of home.

" Looks like they know we are here," Ash screamed pointing the large billboard.

" Looks like you called ahead, couldn't resist the attention. " Emmy says to Maya as Ivan and Lucia defend her.

" I didn't call anyone," Maya defends herself as a driver stepped out of a limo and approached the group.

" Am here for Miss Senn," he asked

" That's me," Maya answered.

" I was sent by your father am suppose to take you to his villa," he said to Maya who was ready to go see him.

Ivan and Ash helped put the suitcases into the car and they were on their way.

Maya was busy calling her mom.

" How could you turn my trip to see my father into business and now the whole world knows am here ? " Maya asked her mother who was laughing.

" Honey we have a business deal with the airline in Egypt and it's great exposure for you, this trip will make the media talk about you more and this will be good for your career," Sophie tried to tell Maya who was angry and she felt dizzy and hanged up on her mother throwing her phone into her bag.

"Woah are you okay ? " Ivan asked his girlfriend.

" I just feel strange its like am changing. " Maya tells Ivan who looked at her and agreed.

" I feel like that sometimes," Ivan tells her as she smiled kissing him as everyone began making fun of them.

" The kissing we can excuse but the whispering off the table and won't be allowed. " Lucia says to pair.

" Guys we are in Cairo and in a limo on our way to a villa can we celebrate that and look out of the window." Emmy asked of the group as they agreed as Maya laughed and they cheered to their friendship since they were kids.

Maya looked out of the window during traffic and the man saw her and looked at her.

He had a grin on his face as his eyes turned shape and Maya was shocked as the man jumped on to a building as the limo got out of the the traffic driving straight to the villa.

Arriving at a security clearance check point and being let into a magnificent neighborhood.

" Looks like daddy is living rich in the suburbs. " Emmy pointed out as Ash shoved her almost making her choke on her drink

Maya was nervous as they arrived.

" Do we go with you inside ? " Ivan asked as Maya asked them let her go ahead.

She walked into the villa and she could hear kids laughing perfectly as she followed the sound to find her father and two young boys playing in the backyard of the home.

" Baba," the boys cried out as Maya looked and saw a strange woman there.

Her heart fell to pieces.

She turned back and went the same way she came in and found her friends standing at the entrance of the home.

" I made a big mistake coming here and I shouldn't have come here," Maya spoke with cracks in her voice.

Connor stopped playing with his son's because he could hear his daughter.

" Maya is here," he announced as Maya could hear him coming.

" Don't go," Ivan said to her.

" I don't want to do this," Maya said pushing him and he fell as Ash and Lucia went to help him and Maya ran off fast before she even noticed she pushed Ivan.

Her father came to find her gone and her friends couldn't keep her from going.

" Mr Senn it's an honor to meet you and your daughter not so much she just pushed Ivan out of her way and ran out of here like lightning." Emmy explained.

Cairo and Omar followed behind their father and everyone was surprised to see them.

" Baba where is our sister ? " Omar asked.

" Cause it's obviously not you." Cairo the smallest said Emmy who was offended.

" I have to go after her this city isn't safe." Connor explained as the group wanted to go with him.

" One missing teen is enough, I don't need the four of you also getting lost, Just stay here and I will be back with my daughter.

Honey get them settled in and give them food." Connor said to his wife Lyla kissing her on the cheek as he went after Maya cause he knew the city was filled with Sha and Lynx.

Maya walking on the streets of Cairo regretting everything and seeing her father with his new family and kids broke her in more ways than anyone could ever imagine.

Sitting on a bench and feeling sorry for herself cause she and her mother were abandoned by her father who now she abandoned her mother for.

Her mother wasn't so villainous anymore and it killed Maya cause her mother was right.

Killed her she had to go home and beg for forgiveness with a tail tucked between her legs.

"Look at you ?

Here feeling sorry for yourself on a bench when you are powerful, a literal goddess. " Maya heard someone vaguely familiar speaking and looked up to see the same guy she saw earlier in traffic.

"You ? " Maya said getting up.

"It's me, I recently woke up from a long nap and the world is not what I left it as, so much to explore and see.

The internet is full of incredible surprises. " The guy spoke strangely.

"Who are you? " She asked.

"I am Seth and I am Sha," he introduced himself with his eyes turning color.

"Sha is that what I am ? " Maya asked with relief something good came out of that day.

"You are no Sha cause you are Lynx and didn't you father tell you what you are ? " Seth asked as Maya looked at him and couldn't answer it.

"I didn't formally introduce myself am Maya."

" It's nice to see you Maya but we are mortal enemies well our tribes." Seth said to her as she wanted to know more.

" I saw a coffee shop, let's go and talk cause I really want to know what's happening to me. Will you join me ? " She asked.

" I have nothing else important to do let's go." Seth answered.

" The Lynx and Sha have been at war for five thousand years and after the first age with bastet's death and Set turned into stone the lynx and sha began to loose their power and transforming was only something the highborns could do and you are a highborn.

You are a Lynx highborn and I am Sha highborn." Seth explained as Maya was confused to what even was a Sha and a Lynx.

" Look at that mirror! " Seth said to her as Maya looked to the mirror right next to their table and it was her looking different.

" Don't worry they can't see it, only Sha and Lynx can see our true forms through a mirror. That is what we are and you are. " Seth whispered.

Maya could clearly see it and it looked like a shadow of a cat Infront of her face and what looked like a jackal Infront of Seth's face.

" Am a cat ! " Maya was shocked as Seth laughed.

" You maybe a cat but you are not like the rest of your kind. " He said taking Maya's hand and placing a kiss on it as Maya smiled and looked to the door as her father walked in the coffee shop and she looked Infront of her and he was gone.

" Maya there you are, I've been looking for you everywhere. " Connor said to Maya who had alot to say to him.

Meanwhile outside the coffee shop Seth watched them with a smile on his face cause he got to her first and now she trusted him.

He was going to get her power and throne much easier and the Sha were going to be on top of the coming war.

Chapter 4

T he ankh or key of life is an ancient Egyptian hieroglyphic symbol used in Egyptian art and writing to represent the word for "life" and, by extension, as a symbol of life itself.

Only a god can hold An Ankh.

A weapon for the Egyptian gods made out of pure gold.

Two Weeks Ago.

A group of worshippers had surrounded Seth's statue praying to him like they always did when the statue began to shake and break.

They were shocked to find a young man underneath the statue of Seth.

" But he's young practically a teenager," whisperers among the worshipers.

The young man looked around and saw people looking at him.

" Get away," he said but they didn't.

" GET AWAY! " he spoke with much authority and fury as they all got away and got on their knees.

" Lord Seth you have returned from stone and back to use," Dan the leader of the Sha spoke.

" Who is Seth ? " The young man asked as Dan was shocked with a sinister idea in his mind.

Present day.

Maya and her father were still sitting in the coffee shop.

"Are you going to speak to me darling ?" He asked.

"What do I say, incredible new family you have here after you abandoned me and my mother." Maya said to him with a sarcastic tone.

"There is so much I have to tell you but I can't tell you and I left you to keep you and your mother safe cause i had to be here and being there risked your lives," he tried to explain.

"Tell me,

I want to know what was so important that I had to grow up without a father,

Do you know all I have had to go through to please mom and make her happy like it was my job cause you broke her and me when you left." Maya lashed out at him.

"Am so sorry my darling daughter, the only thing I could do is watch you from a far and be at every show you have been in. I have followed and watched your very impressive career all these years." Connor revealed to Selene who couldn't help smile.

"You were at my shows ?" Maya asked.

"You could have come to see me," Maya explained.

"It's because they could have seen you and me together and then you would be in danger.

Something I wouldn't allow having those dogs come after you or your mother." Connor placed his hand on the table and he motioned her to look at his hand as they morphed into claws as he scratched the side of the table.

Maya sitting Infront of him with her mouth wide open.

"This is why I couldn't be in your life because I am a lynx, we are the children of Bastet and her warriors, we are heroes and protectors of Egypt.

I was young when I met your mother and I left everything here in Egypt and moved with her to New York where she got pregnant with you and you were perfect in every way but you were not Lynx and the Sha found us one day but I managed to stop them.

More of them would have come after you cause we are currently in a war with the Sha.

I had to leave you with your mother cause you were safer with her in her world than my world." Connor explained to Maya who was still confused.

"Why did you become this way ?

Was it an epidemic ?" Maya asked.

"The early settlers of Egypt used to pray to many gods and it was a different age and the gods walked on Earth and they blessed their worshipers with their power.

Different gods and different powers.

We come from the lineage of Bastet the cat goddess and she gave us the power of speed, Stamina, heightened senses, Strength, we heal much quicker and power to turn into a Lynx Cat cause I am a high born.

Powers beyond anything," Connor explained to Maya who re-called everything she was just told and couldn't believe it still.

"What is this whole highborn thing ?" Maya asked.

"It means am still full of pure Lynx essence and the clowder make us match with another highborn Lynx to produce a much stronger Lynx and your mother is human you can imagine how angry they had gotten." Connor laughed.

" Could they have hurt me ? " Maya asked.

" You are still my daughter even if you aren't one of us and they couldn't harm but they have helped protect you and keep you safe. " Connor finally had explained everything and Maya finally had all the answers she wanted but there was still more she had to know.

She decided to not tell him anything.

" How do you know if one is a Lynx ? Wait for teenage hood or adolescence? " Maya was curious to know.

" We are born with our power and we tested after birth to see if a child has the power of Bastet or not and we use a small shard of Basts amour and if you are one of the Lynx you can touch it but If your human it will burn,

Cause her amour is divine and we are here divine children. " Connor revealed to Maya who was repulsed.

" What was my outcome ? " She asked.

" It nearly burnt you cause once you touched it you cried out as your little hand was red and for children we don't let the babies touch it completely cause we are not monsters. " Connor added.

" What if it didn't burn me and I touched the shard of bastet's amour ? " Maya asked.

" I would have taken you to Egypt and raised you here in Egypt, you will never know how much it hurt me that you weren't like me and that you will never be like me." Connor took Maya's hands into his hands.

" What about my mother what would happen to her? " Maya asked with a cracked voice.

" She knew the risks when we tested you and what it would mean for us, she always knew and knew the sacrifice I had to make. "

Connor shocked Maya who couldn't believe her mother knew and what her mother would have done if she was lynx.

" She knew am not surprised but what if someone develop the Lynx genetics when they were older ? " Maya asked.

" If you think you will become a monster like me then I am happy to tell you no, we are born with our power since birth and becoming a lynx now after being tested and being proven not to be would be highly impossible.

Cause that would mean your DNA changed since birth and DNA doesn't change and the same result you got as a child you will get now.

Unless you are Bastet herself and I would know if my daughter was Bastet." Connor said to her as she laughed.

" you are not a monster, So am not like you what does that mean ? " Maya asked.

" You have to leave but that doesn't mean it has to be tomorrow, stay and get to know me and your brothers and my life, learn our history," Connor pleaded with his daughter who agreed.

" Let's go home before it gets dark," Connor said to her as they got up from their seats and Maya ran and hugged him she left her father paying for the coffee she had ordered before he got there and she ran to the bathroom.

As she washed her hands she felt many emotions of happiness and yet fear but above all new life was starting and the world she thought she knew was not what she knew.

She began to feel something strange as her hands began to glow and a tattoo of an Ankh appeared in her right hand surprising her as she tried to wash it before a giant real life sized Ankh appeared in her hand and she held it and looked at it.

It was Golden with writing on it as she heard the bathroom door open and it disappeared in her hands as she remembered what Seth said to her.

"Your not like the rest of them ? " She remembered as the thought that brought her fear crossed her mind.

Chapter 5

aya and her father returned to the villa and found everyone having a meal prepared by Lyla Amun the wife of Connor.

" I found her," Connor announced as everyone was relieved and happy to see she was okay.

" Are you okay now ? " Lucia asked Maya.

" You pushed me out of the way and your really strong like bodybuilder strong, " Ivan asked Maya who was surprised as her father overheard Ivan and he thought that was surprisingly unique.

" It must have been the floor, " Maya defended.

" Father these are my friends, I don't know if you got introduced but this is Lucia Baker my best friend,

Emmy Kogei my close frienemy and Ash Ramos my best guy friend and Ivan Ryder my boyfriend." Maya introduced.

" Did you say boyfriend ?

Is that something you are allowed to have, " Connor asked as Maya laughed and the boys came running in jumping and tackling their father.

" Boys now is not the time, I brought your sister. " Connor said to them as Maya smiled and was beyond thrilled.

" I always thought I'd die an only child but now I got two baby bros, who are not only handsome but I hear geniuses," Maya asked as the boys were upset.

" Baba why did you tell her," Cairo asked.

" We wanted to make an impression to her," Omar sided with his brother.

" This is Omar Amun Senn he's ten years old and he found a way for us to translate old Egyptian dialect he's our language specialist.

And the youngest Cairo Senn he is a our prodigy, our little engineer and don't let his cuteness fool you he is a fighter beyond his years," Connor revealed as everyone was surprised.

" She is their mother and my wife Lyla Amun," Connor introduced as she came and hugged Maya.

" We are so happy you are here with us, I have heard so many things about you and I can't wait for us to know each other," Lyla said to Maya who didn't mind as the boys took their sisters hand.

" We are going to take her to the wall," they both spoke as Connor smiled seeing all his children together.

" Omar is ten years old and Cairo is age seven, how are they prodigies?" Emmy laughed cause she didn't believe it as Lucia hit her shoulder to keep quiet.

The boys took Maya to a different section of the house that a large wall stood there every magazine that featured her was framed on the wall.

Maya was caught by surprise as was shocked.

" We have collected all of them," Omar said to his sister.

" we buy them and dad frames them," Cairo adds as Maya couldn't believe it.

" This is incredible," Maya gathered her words and spoke.

" This is how we could get to know you but now you are here," Omar says to Maya,

" now am here and you can get to know me," Maya said to her brothers.

That night Maya couldn't sleep as she tossed and turn woke up and got out of bed woke up and wandered the halls of her father's big mansion to find the kitchen and Lyla having a glass of water.

" aren't I happy to finally find another living person, this is a big house." Maya commented.

" It is and sometimes am glad cause I can hide from the boys and relax," Lyla tells Maya who laughs.

" So am I going to call you mom or Lyla ?

Never had a step parent," Maya asked,

" You can just call me Lyla and I hope I can be there for you and if there is anything you need you can come to me, " Lyla assures Maya who appreciated it.

" Tell me are you a Lynx? " Maya asked,

" I am," Lyla answered as she made her eyes turn and fur growing from her skin before she turned back to normal.

" I am a highborn and I was promised to your father but he met and fell in love with your mother and well you know how things went down and when he came back we got married, you see being Lynx comes with sacrifice,

Especially for highborns we have to breed with another and continue the Lynx bloodline," Lyla explained to Maya who was disturbed to learn all that.

" But why ? " Maya asked,

"We are almost going extinct and the war with the Sha is taking making our numbers go less but the main reason is because of Bastet.

Our power comes from her and when she died our people's connection with her began to become less and less to the point some of us forgot and can't even shift,

Last of the people who can shift are your father and Ustet the head of the pride." Lyla explained as Maya sympathized with her.

"But you did love my father ?" she asked.

"I eventually came too and now I have these two wonderful boys who are brilliant and my life," Lyla spoke with Maya and they talked for a few more minutes.

Lyla went back to bed and found Connor on his computer.

"Your daughter is really incredible, all your children are must be a shared gene pool, remarkable like their father," Lyla teased Connor.

"I hope they are nothing like me cause I am an old cat," he said as lyra laughed.

"Your daughter had a unique scent to her, smelled familiar and just superior," Lyla told Connor who laughed.

"My daughter is human remember she's not like us," Connor defended,

"Maybe it's only something a feline can sense," Lyla spoke with a yawn as she went to bed and it left Connor thinking.

"Maya was asking questions and also why did she come to Egypt, " he also remember what Ivan said about being pushed.

He was there when Maya was tested by the pride she couldn't be a lynx.

But what if she was then that would mean,

Connor stopped thinking cause that would be insaine his daughter be Bastet.

Maya returned to her room and found Seth on her bed waiting for her.

" how did you get in here ? " Maya asked.

" cause I have to take you somewhere, you want answers and I will take you to them." Seth said to her.

" Take me where ? " Maya asked.

" To your temple my dear goddess, there your answers await once and for all in the temple of BUBASTIS." Seth said to Maya who trusted him and she wasn't scared to go with him as she took her jacket.

" Keep up," Seth said jumping out of her window and landing on his feet from a two storey building as Maya was terrified and then a part of her just went through and she jumped and landed on the ground safely on her two feet.

" Stamina, agility and speed belong to us," Seth said to Maya as the two began to run and they reached the giant gate and Seth jumped to the other side and when he landed on the ground Maya was standing there waiting for him.

" Look at you such a fast learner," Seth said with a smile on his face.

" am really fast. " Maya was also surprised as Seth had brought his car.

" the temple is only forty minutes away, are you ready ? " He asked as Maya looked at the gate and almost hesitated but then she gave herself courage and went in the car with Seth and they drove off.

Connor came to check up on Maya and found she was gone.

He could smell Sha in her room.

Connor immediately ran to the halls and to a wall where he put his palm and a large red button appeared and he pressed it to alert everyone in the gated community a Sha was close by and they kidnapped his daughter.

The entire community was up and sirens heard from every direction.

" what is it ? " Lyla asked as she and the boys were up.

" what's going on ? " Lucia asked as Ash and Ivan were also awake.

While Emmy was still a sleep.

" A Sha was in her room and they took her," Connor explained as Cairo was terrified as his mother held his hand.

" it's a war they want and it's a war I will give," Connor was upset and his eyes changed as Ivan, Ash and Lucia saw his eyes and they were scared.

" we have to go to the bunker and hide, come on children. " Lyla lead the way as he took everyone to safety and Connor went to group up with the other lynx and go get his daughter.

Chapter 6

The temple of Bubastis (Bohairic Coptic: ⊠⊠⊠⊠⊠⊠⊠ Poubasti; Greek: ⊠⊠⊠⊠⊠⊠⊠⊠ Boubastis or ⊠⊠⊠⊠⊠⊠⊠⊠⊠ Boubastos), also known in Arabic as Tell-Basta or in Egyptian as Per-Bast, was an ancient Egyptian city. a center of worship for the feline goddess Bastet, and therefore the principal depository in Egypt of mummies of cats.

"welcome to Bubastis or should I say your temple,

Before history began, Egypt was the birthplace of all life, A paradise worthy of the gods who created it.

So the gods decided to live here alongside their creation, man.

But there was no mistaking the gods from the mortals who worshipped them.

The gods were different because they could transform into all manner of creatures.

You and I were one of them." Seth said to Maya as they went into the ruins of the temple of Bubastis.

"You are telling me am a god ?

The cat god ? " Maya asked with a chuckle cause she wanted answers but this was madness.

"You wanted answers and here I give them to you, " Seth told Maya as they walked around the ruins.

Meanwhile Connor had assembled a task force to go save his daughter.

"Connor I came as soon as I found out!" Ryan Ustet spoke as Connor was relieved and happy to see his friend.

The leader of the Lynx and the strongest Lynx in the world.

"what is happening?" Ivan asked.

"They are planing on rescuing Maya," Omar answered.

"How did you know that?" Emmy asked,

"super hearing," Omar answered as they group watched from inside the home through the glass wall.

"Who's that?" Ash asked pointing to Ryan.

"The greatest of our kind, Ryan Ustet." Cairo answered as he and his brother could hear the heart beat of Ash go faster.

"I won't stay here while they go out to save my Girlfriend," Ivan spoke as Lyla and Lucia walked in with snacks.

"it's dangerous Ivan, there are forces out there that you can't imagine and only they can face it," Lyla tried to reason but Ivan was hell bent on helping as he went outside to join the lynx taskforce.

"I want to come with you and help find my girlfriend," Ivan said to them as they laughed.

"Who's this?" Ryan asked.

"My daughter's boyfriend, who I admire his courage to save my daughter and I think he should come with us and take her while we kill that filthy Sha that dare take my daughter." Connor said to Ryan and the taskforce as they packed up.

"They were spotted and it looks like they are heading to the Bubastis temple," Ryan confirmed from his sources and was filling them in.

" Temple of Bubastis ? " Connor was confused to why a Sha would be taking his daughter to the temple of Bastet.

" Then let's go, " Ivan spoke to the group as they immediately left and were on their way to the temple of Bubastis.

Meanwhile Maya had learned alot and she couldn't believe it.

" I can't believe I died and I reincarnated, my father Ra the sun god gave me nine lives,

Why nine lives ? " Maya asked,

" represents the nine gods of Egypt, The ENNEAD. " Seth said to her as he stood infront of her and took her hands.

" What are you going ? " Maya asked.

" Am showing you the truth, showing you your power and who you are, " Seth whispered as the Ankh appeared in their hands as they both held it.

" Let's fix up your temple, " Seth said to her as all around them the ruins began to shift and everything began to fix itself and everything was going back to how it was as grass began to grow and water flowing in the ponds as Maya looked all around and everything was beautiful.

What was once a desert had now turned into a utopia.

" this is an Ankh, only a god can hold this weapon, it is life and power and yours to use," Seth explained as he also held on to the ankh.

" if only a god can hold an Ankh then how are you holding on to it with me ? " Maya asked.

" am not just a Sha but I am a god like you. " Seth revealed to Maya who smiled and she felt safe being with someone who understood what she was going through.

" I have to tell you the truth, everything about our history the Sha vs Lynx is a lie and I am not what they say about me, I was set up," Seth said to her as armed men had surrounded them.

" master you brought us Bastet and now we will kill her as many times until her nine lives are over ," Dan the leader of the Sha spoke.

" what are you doing here ? " Seth asked as Maya was confused.

" we are here to do your bidding lord Set," Dan revealed as the men had their guns pointed at Maya who was surprised and disappointed that Seth would do this.

" you brought me here to kill me ? " Maya asked as her eyes turned cat like with fury in them.

" no I didn't bring them here to kill you," Seth defended himself.

" Lord Seth ? " Maya whispered as her father and the Lynx arrived.

" Get away from my daughter or your all dead," Connor yelled as Maya was happy to see her father and wanted to run to him but the Sha still had their guns pointed at her while the lynx had their guns pointed at the Sha.

" Put those guys down," Seth spoke with a growl and his Ankh appeared in his hand and his head turned into a head of his true form a Sha.

" That is set! " Ryan screamed as Connor was surprised.

" impossible set can only rise when Bastet returns ? " Connor spoke as he looked to his daughter who Set allowed her to go to her father.

" you can go to your father," Seth whispered to her as she ran to her father.

" are you okay ? " Connor asked.

" Am fine father," Maya answered,

" I was so worried," Ivan said hugging her as Connor said to take her out of there,

" Ivan what are you doing here ? " Maya asked as Ivan didn't have time to tell her anything and took her out of there and Dan took the moment to shoot Maya,

Seth saw Ivan and Maya,

how they looked at each other,

Looked like love as he wondered what was going on between the two of them and missed Dan as he took his gun out and aimed at Maya and shot her in the neck,

" you bastard," Seth screamed as he turned to Dan and sliced him in half instantly killing him as Maya fell fell to the ground and Ivan caught her as the Lynx began attacking the Sha and a fight broke out.

Maya tried to breath but she couldn't as she looked at saw Ivan begging her to stay calm as Connor on his phone as he was telling Ivan to put pressure on wound.

Maya couldn't breath as she choked on her blood and looked to the side of her eye and saw the shoot out going on as she mastered strength and raised her right hand and the Ankh appeared as Connor and Ivan where in shock.

The Ankh began to glow and it threw out the Sha and Seth along with them, out of the temple and sent them miles and miles away.

Ryan looked and saw what Maya did,

" Bastet ," Ryan knew as Maya dropped her hand as the Ankh disappeared.

Still fighting to stay awake she couldn't fight anymore and she closed her eyes and her heart stopped.

Connor could hear her heart stop and he fell apart crying and holding his dead daughters body as Ivan held her hand with tears flowing down his eyes.

" What is happening to her ? " Ryan pointed out.

Connor looked at his daughter and her neck was regenerating and healing unlike any of the lynx.

Maya was returning to life.

Chapter 7

A month ago

Maya was driving herself home after a long shoot and she was tried but managed to give herself some strength to get home.

When she was backing up a truck came out of nowhere and crushed her car and the impact sent her car flying and immediately combusting into flames with Maya was still inside all cut up and bruised up and she couldn't feel her body and a ringing in her ear.

This was the night Maya died for the first time and it activated her powers.

Maya woke up in her bed and she remembered everything but didn't know how she got in her bed.

She still smelled of gasoline and her clothes were dirty and bloody.

Memories of her injured and burned alive flashed in her mind as she went and took a long hot shower and stepped out of the shower and looked at herself in the mirror and her skin was furry and her eyes were green and cat like.

It scared the life out if her as she went and looked online if there was anyone hurt from the accident and lucky there wasn't and just her car was destroyed.

She knew she could report it stolen or missing but at the moment she was scared and didn't know what she was or how she survived.

Maya opened her eyes and and coughed the bullet out as everyone had witnessed.

"what ? " Maya asked

"your eyes my love," Connor said to his daughter as she turned to Ivan who looked terrified as the men present same reaction.

They knew !

"Maya are you alright? " Connor asked as Ivan helped her to her feet.

"am fine," Maya answered as she pushed her hair out of her face.

"How did your daughter survive that ? " Ryan Ustet asked.

"Nine lives," Maya answered as everyone looked at her and the temple of Bastet was practically brand new.

"All the questions you asked,

And when I told you what I was you weren't scared or shocked, cause you knew," Connor started realising everything was Infront of his eyes this whole time.

"My friend Seth told me that am not just an ordinary Lynx, I am a goddess, I am the incarnation of her," Maya pointed out to a hieroglyph of a cat and Connor looked to it and knew what it means.

"Bastet ! " Ryan whispered as Connor decided they have to return to their Villa and they couldn't stay there anymore cause Set with an army would be on their way back.

When they got home everyone was relieved Maya was safe as her brothers ran to her hugging her as tight as they could.

" am okay nothing bad happened to me," Maya tried to calm her brothers.

" but you were shot and you died and came back to life I don't think you are saying the truth," Ryan meddled as everyone heard what he just said.

" what is your deal ? " Maya asked him.

" am okay," Maya assured everyone.

" I want answers, Connor did you know about this and hide your daughter from the pride so that you would have private access to the goddess Bastet ? " Ryan suggested.

" who is Bastet ? " Ivan asked cause since they left the temple no one told him.

" it's your little girlfriend, at the temple we saw Seth and if he's alive then that means Bastet is here alive in the waking world, " Ryan pointed out as everyone looked at Maya.

" wait you mean she's a goddess ? Like being beautiful wasn't enough for you," Emmy spoke as everyone began to talk.

" this is incredible," Lucia spoke

" how long did you know this ? " Ash also spoke

" our sister is Bastet," Omar said to Cairo as Maya couldn't think properly with everyone talking and asking her so many questions.

" Silence, " Maya roared that echoed through the entire house and everyone was silent as Maya's eyes had changed.

" good, " Maya gathered herself and went to the living room and told them everything of how she died and began to see the changes in her.

" Why did this happen to me also who is Bastet cause I know nothing," Maya asked as her father told her the story.

"Centuries Ago when the world was still brand new and humanity was entering a new age and the gods weren't behind.

They walked on the earth with their creation and it truly was the beginning of a new age,

The Nine main gods of Egypt helped humanity flourish and Egypt was the cradle of civilization before everything fell.

Bastet was the daughter of Ra,

Ra was the sun god and the first pharaoh.

some say Ra is a Titan one of the first beings to walked the Earth.

You see Bastet was to inherit the throne to the Egyptian gods and take her father's place and that would mean she would get his power cause the power of a god doesn't die.

There was one god who was evil and didn't want her to get the throne, his name was Seth.

The god of the desert and famine.

He conspired with his worshippers who he had bestowed his power upon and they were Sha.

Some gods blessed their worshipers with their power and others didn't,

Bastet did and she made her worshippers powerful.

Seth wanted power and he thought he could have it and so he attacked bastet's temple and killed her.

Ra was broken and blessed his daughter with Nine lives like the Nine Ennead,

Bastet was the goddess of life and protection and how did that exactly help her.

Ra died with out ever knowing the fate of his daughter right before cursing Set and Sha to be wonderers and almost powerless.

The Lynx await Bastet for her to claim her throne, kill Apophis before he ends all life and above all stop the Sha who have grown in numbers and are getting organized and seek the death of the Lynx " Connor told the story of Bastet to them.

Maya had tears flowing down her eyes.

She felt pain and sadness.

" Seth ! " Maya said that name again.

" Your new friend is Set cause we saw him holding an Ankh and only a god can hold an Ankh.

He was the one who killed you, Set is evil and the Sha are no exception. " Connor cleared everything for Maya.

" I have to go rest, " Maya excused herself as she went to her room and cried.

" she's in pain, " Ivan was sad watching Maya be sad as they watched her go and the room filled with silence.

Maya was confused and the answers she wanted were not what she expected.

Her life had changed and now she was a goddess and future queen of some throne she didn't want.

Her phone rang and she looked and saw and answered it immediately.

" how are you my love, it's been two days and I haven't heard from you ?

Is everything good or should I come there, " Sophie asks as Maya laughed.

" Mom am fine just some allergies and yes everything is alright, " Maya lies to her mother.

" Am glad to hear that my baby, can't wait to see you soon cause you won't stay there forever you still are a famous supermodel and

I got deals here that will set you up for life," Sophie turned into a manager instead of being a mother.

"I got business to finish here that might take some time and then after that we are going to have a talk cause am sick of people walking over me and killing me. No more !" Maya said hanging up as she wiped her tears.

"I won't be a victim of anyone anymore, not my mother or my father and above all not Seth's and if he wants a war I will give him a war and I will end him and wipe out the evil Sha," Maya was ready to embrace herself and her power and become strong.

This was a new Era for Bastet.

Chapter 8

A day Later,

Maya sat at the edge of the pool just thinking as she watched her family and friends.

"are you okay," Ivan asked sitting next to her.

"Am holding up and I think you all should leave and go back home cause it's not safe here they literally shot me and killed me, I would hate if anything happened to you guys," Maya explained to Ivan who took her hand into his.

"They can go but I will stay with you till the end, I love you Maya and am not afraid to die for you," Ivan confessed and Maya was scared of it reaching that point as she kissed him and he kissed her back.

Connor cleared his throat making the two stop kiss.

"I brought you books on the Egyptian gods and everything we know about Bastet or should I say you," Connor spoke giving them to her as she took them and Ivan helped her read and learn her history more.

There are other gods out there and I got a sister who's a snake, this is extremely strange like I am Bastet and yet I am still me," Maya whispered as Ivan hugged her.

"You are not alone in this, I am here getting through this with you together," Ivan assures her as they continue reading.

The night was approaching fast and Omar and Cairo were sneaking with Emmy, Lucia and Ash out into a private part of the fancy neighborhood a secluded part where all the highborns went to shift and turn into their Lynx form.

"We always come to watch them turn, it's incredible." Omar whispered.

"this is phenomenal," Lucia couldn't believe it as Ash watched Ryan as he undressing and Ryan could sense and he spotted then from a far and he could see Ash looking at him as he smiled.

Ash saw him look directly at him but he didn't stop looking.

"The pride come together to shift and their collective energy makes us stronger and with the Sha drawing closer we need more power." Cairo explained as Emmy was fascinated.

"To be strong and powerful, how does one get such power cause if Maya has this power then why can't I have it," Emmy asked as Omar laughed.

"A human can be turned but the process would be painful and most humans die but only a powerful Lynx can turn you." Omar said to her,

"You want to be a lynx ?" Lucia asked Emmy as they all looked at her to see her answer.

"I want to be powerful," Emmy answered with a devious smile.

They returned to find Maya and Ivan reading.

"Where were you ?" Maya asked.

"They came to watch us shift, something dangerous that humans shouldn't." Ryan reported as Maya was scared for her friends.

"This is why you have to leave," Maya said to them.

"Home I miss home let's go home," Lucia was excited to return.

"Am staying but you all leave tomorrow morning cause it's not safe here and I don't want anyone getting hurt or worse killed," Maya said to her friends.

"We can't leave you here alone," Ash defended.

"The Sha and Seth are out there and all of you are mortal and I will not play with your lives all of will go," Maya said looking at Ivan.

"You made a wise decision daughter cause you have a war to fight and training to begin," Connor voiced his opinion and it was set they were leaving in the morning.

"Such a shame, I thought maybe," Ryan said to Ash as he stopped and walked out as Ash watched him.

That night they spent time and talked and had good food together for what would be their last time together.

The next morning Maya took her friends to the airport.

"what a crazy three day it has been," Lucia remarked,

"It's our fourth day and we are still alive," Maya added as she said goodbye to Lucia and Ash.

"You only got seven lives left, try not to get killed,"Emmy gave Maya last piece of advice as she went into customs and Maya laughed it off.

"Thanks for the advice," Maya laughed as she turned to Ivan who didn't want to go.

"You are valuable to me and I wouldn't let you stay cause if you did am sure you would sacrifice yourself for me and I got seven lives but am sure they would sacrifice yourself for me.

And I can't let you do that," Maya said to him as he kissed her and asked for her to be careful as Seth watched and heard them and he was furious.

Maya watched her friends go in and it felt right as her father and Ryan where there to accompany her but she felt another presence there and looked around and couldn't see anything.

" Let's go back home," Connor said his daughter who had a bad feeling but choose to push it aside and they went back to the villa.

Maya couldn't stop thinking about her friends and was just counting till the hours till the plane landed safely and her friend where completely safe but that didn't happen as a parcel was delivered for them at the door and the boys got it and opened it and they began to scream and call our for their father and sister.

"What is it ?" Lyla asked running to check up on them along with Connor and Maya.

" Look ! " Omar pointed the parcel that was delivered and it was photos.

" They have been kidnapped," Maya took the pictures and looked at each one of them.

Her friends tied up and gagged.

" It's him, " Connor spoke as a phone rang and it was inside the parcel and Maya answered.

" I swear if you touch a single hair on them it's not maya who will come for you but Bastet will and there will be hell to pay, " Maya spoke.

" Nothing will happen to them as long as you listen and follow everything am telling you to the latter or am going to kill your precious mortals and I will begin with your boyfriend," Seth taunted as he watched Maya's friends squirm as they were tied up as he cut the call.

"I have you goddess right in my palms," Seth laughed

Maya distraught as she feared for the life of her friends.

Chapter 9

" They captured us so easily thanks to you Ash," Emmy blamed him as the four where tied up .

" you got a mouth and a temper, " Seth laughed as he walked around them watching them but who he wanted the most was Ivan.

" What does she see in you, mortal and basic as mortals go, " Seth took the blindfold off them with a wave of his finger.

Taking another look at Ivan.

" Don't I know you, cause you look very familiar ? " Seth said looking at Ivan.

" He's not even famous am sure he just got those faces, " Ash defended his friend.

" Thanks bro, " Ivan commented as Seth laughed looking at them.

" So defenseless and weak, do you even know who I am ? " Seth asked as he made his face shift Infront of them.

" You are him, Set. " Lucia spoke shaking.

" You must be Lucia, the one with the knowledgeable and Emmy and Ash and lastly my favorite Ivan. " Seth remembered their names.

" I apologize for my followers kidnapping you, but you see am a god and kidnapping mortals is beneath me but I don't want you,

I want her.

She's the only thing I want actually, " Seth explained to them.

" You better stay away from her, " Ivan yelled.

" Or what mortal , you will kill me " Seth laughed.

" Even Ra couldn't kill me, " Seth added as took a chair and sat Infront of them as he made his Ankh appear in his hands as Emmy was giving him eye signals making him smile.

Before he closed his eyes and the Ankh began to glow.

Meanwhile Maya was devastated and feared for her friends as her father was waiting for her and he had a sword.

" what is this ? " Maya asked.

" short and quick training, you have to be able to call on the Ankh which is your power and use it to defend yourself and if that fails use your instincts.

Your strength, stamina and speed. " Connor couldn't help but make it very clear so that Maya knew the danger she was facing as he came at her with the sword and jumped above him and she raised her hand and her ankh appeared as her father smiled but wasn't letting her out of the hook and attacked her and she used her Ankh to slice her father's blade and deflect him with a small blast .

" Very good," Connor was proud as he got up.

" my memories are coming back slowly by slowly," Maya said as she picked up what was now two halves of the blade and fixed it.

" incredible," Connor was glad as he asked her to find them.

Maya closed her eyes and her ankh appeared Infront of her and she opened her eyes and they where cat like and she could see everything as her eyes wandered looking for her friends to find them tied up in an abandoned warehouse but Seth saw her.

"you have already learned the power of sight, I guess you are coming," he smirked as Maya returned to her body.

"She's coming ," Seth said to his captives as Maya was really on her way .

"I have a view on the warehouse is everyone ready?" Maya asked as she was six buildings away.

"where are you ? " Ryan asked through her ear piece as they where near the warehouse in vans.

"am up enjoying the view," Maya said to him as she stood at the edge of the building and she felt fearless and the world was in her hands as she jumped from building to building, running as fast as she ever could and now it was ten times that of a mortal.

Jumping through the room and down to where Seth had her friends.

"Maya or should I say Bastet ! " Seth welcomed as Maya eyes turned green before going back to normal.

"am here let them go," Maya told Seth.

"they leave when I want you them to leave," Seth screamed as Maya didn't like his tone and she made her ankh appear.

"talk to me like that again and you will know that I am my father's daughter," Maya said to him as he apologized.

"you are a goddess I shouldn't speak to you that way, especially after the history we have together. " Seth added as Maya was surprised and it made her Ankh disappear.

"I need to talk to you and it's urgent," Seth said to her as the lights went out and they heard screams as Maya couldn't see anything and when their vision came back Lucia was stabbed and bleeding from her mouth still tied up.

"you," Maya screamed as looking at Seth.

"I didn't do anything, I didn't even move," Seth defended himself as Maya attacked him with all her might and Connor and Ryan came in with the lynx back up freeing them and helping poor Lucia.

"There are other forces at play here," Seth defended as he turned into a Sha jackal and disappeared as Maya went back to check up on Lucia to find her bleeding out.

"can you save her ?" Ivan asked as Maya didn't know how to as she turned to look at her father who didn't know.

"Am a god I can save her ?

Right ? " Maya asked frantically.

"You are not a full god right now you are currently half mortal," Connor reasoned with his daughter as she made her Ankh appear and began to concentrate and tried to save Lucia but it didn't work.

Lucia breathed her last as she died in Maya's hands and she screamed.

Everyone couldn't believe it Emmy was comforted by Ash who both where petrified.

Connor was heartbroken seeing a young girl dead and his hate for Seth and the Sha only grew and just like that the war had began.

Maya held on to Lucia as she cried for her best friend and sister.

Seth watched from a far and he knew a force was out there trying to flame the fire of war and they had just got it and the Lynx would be coming from the Sha and the Sha would not sit idly by and death was coming.

Chapter 10

Maya watched as Lucia's body was taken back to Metro city and she and her friends had to go home.

Her family was devasted but the real cause of death was hidden not to raise unwanted attention.

Maya had to leave her father and brothers behind and Ryan Ustet returned with them back to Metro city.

"what is the point of having all these lives and being a goddess when all I can do is watch someone I love die," Maya asked Ivan who didn't have an answer.

"you have to take the pressure of yourself, you just came into your power and you need time to get better and soon they will never hurt you or anyone else." Ivan said to her as she rested her head on his shoulders as the plane was about to take off.

Emmy was off hooking up with a random guy in the bathroom.

Ryan got a seat next to Ash.

"you okay?" Ryan asked.

"no am not okay, watched my friend get murdered am heartbroken and angry and a mixture of emotions," Ash answered looking out the plane window as Ryan took his hand into his entwining them together.

"nothing will happen to you while am here," Ryan assured Ash.

Ten hours later they had arrived and landed in Metro city and Maya found her mother waiting for her at the airport running to her and getting embraced.

" am so sorry baby," she whispered to Maya as she saw Ryan.

" who's he ? " She asked her daughter.

"Mother this is Ryan Ustet and he's hear to protect us but mostly me and after the funeral we go back to Egypt, there is so much I have to tell you," Maya said to her mother who was surprised to what was happening.

" am going home ," Emmy spoke out.

" I thought we are all going to my place," Maya asked.

" we are in Metro city and I live in a secured apartment, we can split up and go to our homes and see our families.

We can meet at the funeral tomorrow," Emmy reasoned.

" you can come stay with me Ryan ! " Ash offered as he lived in the same building with Maya and he agreed.

Ivan kissed Maya goodbye as he to left and they sort of split up.

Maya went home to finally tell her mother what was happening.

" tell me what's happening? " Sophie hill asked.

" I found out am the incarnation of the goddess Bastet," Maya spoke as her eyes shifted and they were cat like and she made her Ankh appear in her hands.

" we tested you as a kid how is this possible," Sophie was surprised as Maya told her everything.

Meanwhile Emmy arrived at her apartment and found Seth there.

" you came back for more, I thought I satisfied you at the plane bathroom, " Emmy spoke jumping on him and kissing him as he stopped for a second to talk.

" I need information, is there another god Maya has been in contact with? " Seth asked.

" everything is Maya this and Maya that, what about what I want ? " Emmy asked,

" well what do you want ? " Seth asked.

" I want power just like yours to become a Sha obviously, to be powerful," Emmy answered and Seth was impressed and he made his hand shift and his claws and he took her hand scratched her, a deep cut that went clean inside and black veins began to spread all over her bodies as she fell to the floor in pain screaming in pain.

" The transformation is usually pain full and most mortals don't even make it through, am curious to see if you survive," Seth laughed watching her.

Back at the Hill apartment,

Sophie couldn't believe what had happened to her daughter.

" am so sorry for everything," it was the first time Sophie Hills was sincere and that night Maya couldn't help but think of the other gods.

She clearly needed help but she didn't know how to find them and it was a lost cause.

The next day arrived Lucia was buried in her family cemetery and Maya was still in alot of pain and she didn't see Emmy at the funeral as she and Ivan went to her home only to find she had never got there and they went to her apartment and found her and she looked different.

" are you okay ? " Ivan asked,

" just got the twenty four bug I will be okay ," she lied as she pretended to ignore Maya and Ivan who left and Seth appeared from the shadows and asked Emmy again.

" is there another god Maya has talked to ? " He asked,

" no why ? " Emmy asked.

" because there has to be another god pulling strings, " Seth explained an idea he had.

" Why ? What do you mean ? " Emmy asked.

" I didn't kill your friend and it couldn't have been Maya, remember our vision was taken and we went completely blind and your friend was stabbed, it was the work of god cause no mortal could have killed her, " Seth fully explained what he was thinking.

" if you didn't do it then who did ? Who is this other god ? " Emmy finally caught up.

" That's why you have to be my eyes and ears and find out who is this and you can't tell them, whoever this god is they are powerful and they could kill you in a blink of an eye and who knows they could be really close, " Seth added as Emmy was in to avenge Lucia's death.

Maya and Ivan where about to get in a taxi when everything froze and the entire world went silent and Maya looked around and everything had stopped moving.

Birds in the sky, children across the street playing and even Ivan.

" Bastet ," Maya heard her name and turned to see a woman standing in the middle of the road fully moving.

" I have come to take you home sister," the woman spoke revealing her god self.

" I know you ," maya approached her .

"you do, now the other gods are waiting for you." The woman said to Maya.

"The other gods," Maya was surprised.

"the great Ennead is waiting," the woman extended her hand and Maya took it and they shot into space as everything started moving again and Ivan looked next to him and Maya was gone as he looked around and ran to the middle of the road calling out for "Maya".

Chapter 11

" The Ennead or Great Ennead was a group of nine deities in Egyptian mythology worshipped at Heliopolis.

The nine shifter gods.

The main powerful gods were responsible for much of Egyptian civilization.

We are the ones who protected the mortals, made the land fertile and the weather livable and Heald their sick, we did alot," the mysterious woman explained to Maya.

" so what did the gods get from all the worship? " Maya asked.

" more power and invincibility, now do you remember me? " She asked as She looked into Maya's eyes and Maya into hers.

Her snake eyes,

" Renenutet my sister," Maya remembers.

The first time she recognized someone from her first life.

" I now go by Rene," she smirked as all around them started to materialize.

" where are we? " Maya asked.

"We are in A'Aru (The Field of Reeds) or the afterlife, it's where we live, it's where the mortals come to begin their journey and reincarnation.

Cause you see all life is sacred and gets to live again, the cycle of Ra," Rene reminded Maya who looked around and couldn't believe it.

It was a utopia.

"We are beings of life that's why we all carry ankhs, so the only place fitting for us is the afterlife but once it was Earth before you died anyway," Rene began walking as Maya followed her.

" so we can bring back to life my friend ?" Maya asked as Rene stopped her.

"We can't bring anyone to life only Ra he's that kind of power, our father but he's dead," Rene revealed as Maya only knew half of the information.

" That is our temple and our home, your home Bastet. " Rene revealed as Maya's breath was taken away.

Magnificent pyramids made of gold unlike anything she had ever seen as they went inside and once inside Rene took her god form and waited for Bastet to take hers.

" I can't do that," Maya responded as Rene was surprised.

" You still haven't unleashed the god within you but soon you will," Rene said to Maya with a devious smile as they went inside the pyramid, and on the inside the walls were full of hieroglyphs.

" what are all these drawings? " Maya looked around.

" The history of our births and many prophecies, we are primal beings, children of RA the titan god he breathed life into most of us, and others were born from human believing, and that belief birthed them.

We are nine of the main gods but there are many other gods out there because as long as people have faith there will always be a god, " Rene explained and Maya was surprised.

" so it's you and me leaving seven other gods, " Maya smiled.

" Yes, let's go meet them, " Rene winked as they went to the grand hall where nine thrones stood, and above them stood an even bigger throne.

But one of the thrones was destroyed.

" she's here, " Rene whispered as the gods began to appear all around the room in front of their thrones.

Maya looked around the room she was standing before gods and they were in their true forms, beings of absolute power.

Maya looked at them and she would remember them.

" khepri, Thoth, sobek, khnum, we are few? " Maya thought out loud.

" Ra is dead and Seth well he's on earth and Shezmu he's forsaken, Thoth explained as Rene laughed.

" Ra my father," Maya remembered him.

" He left you his throne and his power. You are his successor." Rene revealed that Maya didn't want it.

"Am just nineteen years old I can't take over for Ra," Maya replied as they laughed.

" you haven't shed your mortal form, only once you are a god then you can sit on it, " Rene explained.

" Have you sat on it? " Maya asked as the gods all looked to Thoth.

" I tried to take a seat and it electrocuted me," Thoth confessed as they laughed at him.

" for the god of wisdom you are very foolish at times," Rene remarked as Maya tried to recap.

" You are the god of wisdom, your true form is an ibis," Maya tried to sum it up.

" I am the god of rebirth, "Sobek the crocodile god spoke.

" I am the lord of the air, "Khepri the scarab god revealed.

" Khnum is the lord of the Earth the bull god and I am the god of love," Rene summed it up.

" I know I am the god of protection and love and Seth of the desert and Ra a freaking sun god but who is Shezmu? " Maya wondered.

" He was an old god, he never chose a form like the rest of us and he was an abomination but we stopped him a long time ago, " Rene assured Maya who was relieved.

" The only problem I have on my hands is Seth and I want him stopped can I count on you to help me stop him?

He killed my friend who I now learn no one can bring back to life when we are literal gods," Maya went on a rant as they agreed after a few moments of silence.

" let's go party then, "Khnum screamed as the others cheered.

" Party right now? " Maya was surprised.

" We are gods and mortals issues we don't get mixed with," Khnum said to Maya.

" We go to the mortal realm to party as long as we leave one of us here in this realm to protect the afterlife from apophis devouring everything, " Khepri revealed.

" I will stay as usual, " Thoth volunteered.

" Let's go have some fun," Sobek cheered as he took Maya carrying her in his arms and teleporting away with her Khnum and Khepri followed and Rene was about to follow but Thoth stopped her.

" Why didn't you tell Bastet that Shezmu is alive and closer to her than ever before, he killed her friend and that's why you went for her to bring her where she would be safe! " Thoth reminded her.

"We have to protect her besides she is still mortal right now and that's why she can't even sense Shezmu, but I will awaken her full god powers and she will sit on that throne," Rene pointed at it.

" don't worry and is there anything else? " Rene asked,

"What of Seth? She has to be the told the truth that Seth and she were lovers meaning he would never hurt her or kill her, " Thoth asked as Rene remembered that part of the story.

" I will sneak out and go visit Set, everything will be okay. Ra knew it that's why he gave her nine lives to return and finally fix everything and restore us and our power. Returning us to what we were," Rene knew a new age for them was coming soon and Bastet was the key to getting them there.

To be continued.......

Chapter 12

"It's time to go Feral my dear Bastet, if there is one thing we love it's a good party and back in ancient Egypt we used to give the mortals parties to remember

And they loved it and us,

We also loved partying with the mortals," Sobek explained.

"You must be the party animal of the group," Maya asked as Khepri looked to her and nodded.

Maya looked out of the window and saw they where in New York city up above the empire state building.

"incredible," She whispered

"We know now let loose and become feral," Sobek said to Maya as her eyes where cat like and Sobek held his hand out for her and she took it joining him on the dancefloor.

Rene arrived at the club to find khepri and khnum seated having drinks.

"Where is Maya ?" She asked them as Khepri pointed out to the dance floor.

"I will watch out for her do what you have to do ?" khepri assured Rene as he knew what she was up to thanks to his all seeing eye.

"won't take long," Rene spoke as she vanished.

To appear back in Metro city at an apartment.

Looking around to find clothes on the floor and followed the trail to a bedroom were she found Emmy naked on the bed with Seth sleeping.

She looked at them and laughed as Emmy could smell Rene and woke up jumping to attack Rene who turned into her god form and Emmy punched her only to break her hand as Rene smirked before throwing Emmy across the room but Emmy got up and growled like a Sha as Seth woke up to stop the fight.

" you turned this poor girl into a Sha ? " Rene couldn't believe it.

" she asked for it," Seth answered.

" plus you are also sleeping with her, does Bastet know," Rene looked at Seth who looked down as Emmy was all healed.

" you messed my house," Emmy complained.

" mortals and their simple problems," Rene scoffed as she waved her hand around the room and everything was fixed.

" a god ? " Emmy realized.

" The Goddess Renenutet Hathor, goddess of love." Seth explained to Emmy as Rene was seated on the couch.

" Am here to talk you, " Rene asked Seth who went to sit with her.

" Can you leave the room darling, the gods are taking, " Rene rudely asked Emmy who wasn't going to move.

" As if, you move bitch, " Emmy remarked as Rene's eyes turned that into a snake and she was morphing into one as Seth stopped her and got up and took Emmy to the bedroom.

" Just stay in here, you don't know who that is and what she could do to you, don't piss of a god especially when she's the goddess of love, " Seth pleaded with her.

" she doesn't look that scary ? " Emmy asked,

" Well she is terrifying and unstable and she is super dangerous, she's bastet's sister," Seth explained as he begged her to stay in the room and Emmy agreed.

Seth returned to Rene who sat in the living room to wait for him.

" Am glad you took care of her before I cut off her nasty tongue or worse banished her to the underworld forever with no love," Rene thought as Seth laughed.

" you haven't lost your touch," Seth complimented as Emmy could hear everything in the room.

" why are you here ? " Seth asked,

" am here to tell you to back off Bastet or should I say Maya, she's our now and I will help her become the successor my father knew she would be." Rene explained as Seth knew what she talked about.

" let me guess you will help her rule ? " Seth asked as Rene laughed at his small minded reasoning.

" I will rule," she answered with a devious smile.

" Bastet was no idiot and she will find you out and stop you! " Seth threatened Rene.

" No we will stop you and the entire Ennead will come for you," Rene threatened back.

" You mean you, Thoth, Khepri, khnum and Sobek, together you are not as strong or powerful as you once where ! " Seth laughed at her.

" We got Bastet and she will return our former glory answer will be just as dangerous as we have always been and we will come for you first cause she's pissed at you for killing her friend, " Rene revealed as Seth stopped her and told her he didn't.

"Interesting so we were right, you didn't kill her so that means it was really him.

He's back," Rene revealed.

"another god ?" Seth asked,

"Not just any god but the forsaken, you remember him," Rene reminded him as Seth was speechless.

"Thought we stopped him ?" Seth remembered.

"When it comes to him nothing you remember you can trust even your mind and what it tells you or reminds you." Rene whispered to him as she stood up.

"Stay way from Maya and everyone she loves cause if another person dies then you die and watch out for him, he could be anywhere," Rene final words before she vanished again returning to the club to find Maya partying and having a fun time.

Who was Rene not to join in as well as they partied away for hours.

"Ennead can you hear me ?

I sense there is a creature there and you are all in danger ! " Thoth called out to the gods.

"Was that Thoth in my mind talking to me ?" Maya asked as she stopped dancing and Sobek froze the entire room filled with mortals and they stopped moving.

Rene looked around and cause she could smell sand and rotting corpses.

Maya looked around as Rene and khnum joined them as Sobek concentrated on making the room freeze.

"We have to go," Sobek told the group as Khnum looked around and he couldn't see khepri.

" we have find him," khnum whispered as he ran off to find khepri as Rene looked to Sobek and they turned into their god forms as Maya saw something moving amongst the crowds as she moved closer and saw a creature wrapped in bandages as it came charging to her as she called for her Ankh and placed a protection on her throwing the creature away.

" we have to go and get you out of here," Sobek said to Maya as she said no until khnum and Khepri returned and before they could go Maya saw a figure in the shadows looking at her as it laughed at them and the other gods heard it as they all left and returned back to the A'Aru the field of reeds or the afterlife.

" He was there wasn't he ? " Thoth asked as Rene looked away.

" The forsaken, " Maya answered as she looked to his broken throne.

" Shezmu is back, " Rene revealed.

Chapter 13

T en Thousand years Ago,

Ancient Egypt a great evil was rising, a threat that threatened the mortals and gods.

Ra being the sun god could not leave the A'ARU cause he had to protect all life from there and so he sent the great Ennead to stop this threat.

To stop one of their own, Shezmu had become a god killer.

He had gone to far and he was sacrificing other gods and mortals to increase his power and had built a temple and a mass of devoted legion of worshipers.

He was almost becoming unstoppable.

Bastet led the rest of the Ennead to stop him and it wouldn't have happened if it wasn't for the mortals she and Seth bestowed their power in.

Shezmu was obsessed with power and wanted to become greater than a Titan or Ra himself.

Power hungry.

The mortals now Sha and Lynx helped the gods and wounded him for the gods to finally come in and finish him.

Bastet cursed him to become wild without a form and never have worshipers and be forgotten from history.

Rene took his powers for all the pain he had inflicted on the mortals and fellow gods he had butchered to grow his power cause after all he was the god of death and he couldn't be killed.

"Do you see why Shezmu is dangerous, last time it took seven gods to put him down and that's why I have to go and become Bastet," Maya explained to her mother, Ivan and Emmy along with Ash and Ryan.

She was also on the phone on a video call with her father and brothers.

"while we also have Seth out here, it's a mess and I don't want anyone to get killed," Maya said to them.

"You need training to become powerful and once you are we will be protected," Sobek explained as he and Rene where also in the room.

"why are you here again," Ivan asked.

"To protect Bastet her power is growing and if we could sense her then Shezmu can or Seth," Rene explained.

"That's why am going, don't know how long or when I will be back," Maya almost cried as she looked to her mother who couldn't believe this was her daughters life.

"I need to speak to you," Ivan got up taking Maya's hands to another room to talk.

"I don't want you to leave," Ivan pleaded.

"He's very interesting he got an aura around him, how did they meet ?" Rene asked,

"He was a photographer and they that's how they met," Emmy answered as Rene had not revealed she was with Seth in her apartment.

" I thought they met at the subway and went to the same school? " Sophie wondered as Rene could see everyone was remembering something different.

She found it odd.

Maya in the room with Ivan and things where not going well.

" I think we should break up, you see I have changed and I now I choose to focus on myself," Maya explained.

" it's that Sobek guy, but he's a crocodile," Ivan reasoned as Maya laughed.

" But am a lioness and it's not to with him but for myself, I want to find everything about myself, discover the good and bad, I want to discover Bastet. " Maya reasoned with him as he was broken.

" I understand and I will always love you," Ivan assured Maya who kissed his cheek.

" am glad you don't hate me," Maya smiled as they stepped out of the room and she hugged her mother.

They had their final family dinner together as the gods watched them and were touched.

Maya spoke to her brothers and father over video chat and Connor was to send a special group of lynx protectors to protect Sophie and Ryan was going to stay around to protect them and be with Ash.

Maya went to her bedroom and looked at it, all the memories in it.

She smiled and then began to pack a few clothes before she felt Seth praying to her as he summoned her to him.

" You evil piece bastard, you killed me and also killed my friend ," Maya yelled at him.

" How many times do I have to tell you am innocent, I have been putting things together, someone has been messing with us from the begining.

You and I loved each other and we where going to begin a dynasty of gods but he managed to get his power, cause do you remember what happened to you ? " Seth asked.

" I can only remember few moment, I was in your arms and you where crying." Maya remembered.

" But Ra punished you and it turned you petrified," Maya wondered.

" His power is manipulation, and he could have manipulated history and us, what if when we stopped him he managed to get his power back," Seth pleaded as he took Maya's hands.

" I loved you and still love you, you where the water that quenched my desert, I would never hurt you. I now remember, I came to save you that fate full day," Seth told Maya who could see the sincerity in his eyes.

" you are telling the truth," Maya said looking into his dark eyes.

" He made our races fight and kill each other all these decades that you where not here and I was stone ." Seth made her finally see.

" if this has been Shezmu this entire time then he's dangerous than we ever thought," Maya thought out loud as Seth smiled kissing her and Maya could see his memories and how he plotted with Emmy and was having sex with her and worse Turing her into Sha.

" You are disgusting, stay away from me," Maya pushed him.

" growing powerful I see, whatever you saw I can explain," Seth tried to reason.

" seducing my friend, turning her into a Sha, to turn on me ? Your evil has no bounds and this has all been you, your manipulative and a lair and you will pay Set! I will come for you, " Maya threatened as she returned back to her room and didn't even pack came out of the room and announced she was ready as Rene and Sobek couldn't be happier.

Maya said goodbye to everyone and her mother.

" will you be okay ? " Sophie asked with a worry look.

" mom I don't want you to worry about me, I want you to be brave and fearless for me," Maya spoke to here as her eyes changed and her mother's eyes just like hers.

" I will be brave and not worry," Sophie repeated as Maya hugged her left with the gods to go to A'Aru to beging her god training.

Everything had changed and Maya was finally on the path Ra designed for her.

Emmy returned to her apartment and found Seth waiting for her.

" Leaving ? " She asked.

" correction we both are," Seth told her.

" where to ?"

" we are going home to Egypt, I am a god after all and leader of the Sha and from there I can plot and with my army we will stop Shezmu cause I believe he's out there and he is alive and well, " Seth believed as Emmy asked why.

" To protect Bastet, " Seth answered her.

" you love that social climbing model ? " Emmy asked as Seth laughed.

" I love her like Ra loved the earth and she is my heart and my paradise in the middle of the desert and nothing in this world can ever compare to Bastet, she is a diamond,

a goddess,

A real woman is what she is and everything you are or any other woman is will never stand even close to what Bastet is, " Seth slowly whispered to Emmy as she shed a tear with a heart full of pain and anger.

" Lets go, " he said to her as she wiped her tears.

" I hate you Maya, " she confessed in her heart.

Meanwhile in a dark alley Rene appeared but in a human form to meet none other than Shezmu.

" your are the master of shadows, bleeding into her life and when they find out the great evil Shezmu was actually once great but now my slave," Rene laughed as she bit her finger looking at him.

" She soon will be become a full god and you will have to kill her seven times and no daddy here to save my baby sister,

This time she remains dead like she was suppose to be in the first place, be prepared and don't kill anyone else just yet cause I want her to unlock her full power, " Rene ordered Shezmu who was a part of Maya life and really close to her.

Your probably wondering who Shezmu is disguised as but you know.

Ten thousand years ago the Ennead did strip Shezmuz power and he was evil but his evil was nothing compared to Rene who hated her sister for being their fathers successor and all powerful.

Rene found Shezmu in the wilderness a few thousand years later and enslaved him to her.

Cause she is the goddess of love and as long as there is love in your heart you are a slave to her.

She sent Shezmu to kill Bastet.

She had been watching over Maya for months and tried to kill Maya in the car crash was her doing and the gun shot that killed Maya in Egypt, Rene was literally there whispering in the armed mans ear.

She always been there waiting to get Bastet.

Only a few more lives till Bastet would be dead for good.

Rene held on to her sister as they where in the A'Aru watching the souls cross over into the after life.

" You are going to be okay, I will take care of you baby sister," Rene assured Maya stroking her hair as she held onto Maya's head on her lap with the other gods enjoying the view.

" I've got big plans for you Bastet and this time no one is saving you from me," Rene said to herself as it was only just the beginning.

Chapter 14

R a (/r□□/ transliterated r□w /□□i□□uw/; cuneiform: □□ ri-a or □□ri-ia Phoenician:]5[,□□romanized: r□) or Re (/re□/; Coptic: □□, romanized: Rē) the ancient Egyptian deity of the sun.

By the Fifth Dynasty, in the 25th and 24th centuries BC, he had become one of the most important gods in ancient Egyptian religion, identified primarily with the noon-day sun.

Ra ruled in all parts of the created world: the sky, the earth, and the underworld.

He was the first pharaoh of Ancient Egypt. He was the god of the sun, order, kings and the sky until he vanished.

Maya read in the great library as Rene was with her making sure she was learning.

"I know all this already," Maya complained as Rene told her to keep reading.

The next few days Maya kept reading and training and Rene could see it was taking slower and there was no any progress.

"Thoth found a spell to make you relive your life and walk in those shoes again and finally see who you where cause that's who we need," Rene rudely said to Maya.

"Harsh," Sobek mumbled and Rene knew it was wrong of her and apologized.

" it's okay, am also exhausted of being powerless and I want to unleash my power and become stronger," Maya answered as she got up and went to Thoth who gave her a scroll and she opened it and it glowed bright as Maya closed her eyes to open them to find herself in the middle of the desert surrounded by the Nine gods.

The Great Ennead was united.

" Bastet," Ra called for her.

" Ennead I called you here to tell you I have seen my death," Ra said to them as they all where shocked.

" Father you are Ra, the sun god how can you possibly die ? " Rene asked him.

" I have lived a millennia and a thousand life times, I know every soul by every name, I have survived the titans, my death is written in stone," Ra broke the news to them as he took Bastet's hand.

" I saw my death that is true but then I also saw my daughter take my place and rule Egypt and evolve into something we as gods have yet to become," Ra said to Bastet as the other gods where in utter shock and Rene was upset and she knew what her father was going to say.

" I make you heir Bastet, you will take my power and rule the gods of Egypt and Egypt itself, I have seen your heart and it is the heart of a true Queen," Ra spoke to her as Maya looked around and saw the gods celebrate her and congratulate her as the gods where half beast and men.

Seth was there and he looked dashing when he was still a god and Shezmu was also there and he looked like a cross breed of almost all animals.

Maya was in awe of everything.

" Walk with me my Bastet," Ra called out as Maya went with him and she could see the city from a mile away.

" It's beautiful isn't it ? " Ra asked.

" It's very beautiful, " Bastet answered as they stopped and he turned to look at her.

"Bastet what clouds your mind ? " Ra asked.

" You have given me such a burden, how can i ever take your place and become a fraction of the pharaoh you are. " Maya tells him as he laughs.

" You should have chosen Rene, She's older and she should be your successor ! " Maya spoke out as Ra looked at her and smiled.

" To a great leader is to be selfless, kind and loving and those are the traits you are, to be a pharaoh one must carry all those three in their heart." Ra said to Maya.

" What if am not powerful enough ? " she asked.

" You will be cause I have seen it all and you my dear Maya will accomplish everything I couldn't," Ra spoke as Maya was surprised.

" You just called me Maya ?

You know ? " She asked.

" I know you are Bastet from the future and I know what happens to you and me," Ra openly confessed.

" Then why don't you change things and stop my death ? " Maya asked.

" Because every gods life is a journey and for who you will become we can't change anything, because everything that happens to you changes the world forever." Ra tells her as he took her hands and kissed them.

" Your power is only your and you alone can control it, take it and use it, " Ra tells Maya who closed her eyes and began to channel her power and she finally could tap into Bastet in her full glory and opened her eyes to see Rene standing Infront of her.

" Are you ready to finally begin your training? " Rene asked her younger sister.

" I am, " BASTET ANSWERED.

Chapter 15

Seth and Emmy had returned to Egypt and they where in search of someone who practiced the ancient arts of Heka.

"Her name is Sonja and she is a mystical witch," Seth explained.

"What's so different about Heka and Magic?" Emmy asked.

"Magic comes a gifted individual who is a homo Magus and Heka is ancient Arts taught to a few mortals by various gods." Seth explained as Emmy was intrigued.

As they saw a woman standing out in the desert alone.

"Lord Seth," Sonja greeted as she bowed.

"You came with another Sha here?" Sonja asked.

"Well she wanted to tag along and see more of this world," Seth explained as Sonja didn't understand.

"She recently turned into Sha," Seth explained as Sonja now understood looking at Emmy and seeing the change happening.

"I see the humanity leaving your body, when you die you return to lord Seth and he will get even more stronger," Sonja explained as Emmy turned to look at Seth.

"My power will return to me that you have inside you," Seth explained as Maya had fully understood.

Seth turned to Sonja to ask her for help.

" I need you to summon Shezmu for me, I feel he is near and wants to harm Bastet," Seth explained.

" Shezmu the forsaken, he might kill me for calling on him," Sonja refused.

" If you do this for me then I will be in dept to you and am a god we never forsake those who do right by us," Seth spoke as his Ankh came out his hand and Sonja looked at it and Seth eyes.

She agreed.

" Let's begin, " she said as Seth and Emmy followed her to her cave and she got a fire started and asked for a living sacrifice.

" Shesmu is the lord of Death and the only way to call him is by bloodshed and death," Sonja explained as Seth looked to Emmy and she got scared.

" You called me here to kill me ? " Emmy got sacred as Seth laughed pointing behind her as she turned to look and saw a calf.

" I summoned it, I heard rumours that Shezmu original form was a cow and this might piss him off enough to show up," Seth explained as Sonja immediately killed it and very brutal.

Throwing the cows heart into the fire and the blood of the cow she used it to draw a circle.

" Shezmu Lord of Death, we summon you with blood and death, show yourself to us we are but your humble servants. We pray to you," Sonja prayed as she began a tribal dance around the fire as the fire burst growing bigger.

" What next? " Emmy whispered to Seth.

" We wait for him," Seth explained.

Meanwhile in New York Ivan was walking down an alley when he heard the prayer and could smell the smoke of the burning heart.

Someone praying in my honor, he couldn't believe it and he disappeared to go see who was praying for him.

"I am here my child you prayed and I came," Ivan spoke as he looked around to see the old woman Sonja and a big fire and the two.

"Ivan," Both Emmy and Seth shocked to see him.

"Shezmu, it's always been you," Seth believed it as he always had suspicions.

"I can be anything and anyone," Shezmu answered.

"Lies,

it was always you, I didn't kill Lucia but that's way you and the day Maya got shot in the face that was you as well cause where a death happens you are always there," Seth added it all up as Ivan clapped his hands.

"You weren't just a pretty face but intelligent as well but am sure not as intelligent to know who is behind all this," Ivan laughed.

"Who is it ?" Seth asked.

"Dangerous forces are at play and have been since the beginning." Ivan explained.

"Since the beginning?" Emmy couldn't understand.

"The murder of Bastet that I was framed by you and am guessing that was you," Seth yelled.

"Bastet has many enemies in high and low places, I am just a slave," Ivan spoke as the entire cave began to shake and the fire turned green.

"Another god is here." Sonja announced as a dark cloud fell upon Ivan as he was finally glad they knew as he disappeared.

"summon him back," Seth yelled.

" This other god is powerful and is shielding him from my heka," Sonja explained.

" I can't believe it this entire time it was Ivan, he is the one behind this all, " Emmy couldn't believe it.

" He just forces are at play and he's just a slave, so there is someone out there much dangerous who pulling the strings," Seth explained.

" What do we do with this information ? " Emmy asked Seth.

" I unite the Sha and Lynx and we get our revenge," Seth swore.

Chapter 16

Six months had gone by, Maya was excelling in her training she was getting powerful and learning more of her self with each passing second.

she was almost ready.

" You are almost ready," Rene told Maya.

" ready to fight Seth and his Sha ? " Maya asked cause she hadn't forgiven Seth for all he did to her.

Killing her friend and her or so she thought.

" No to take our fathers throne and became a living goddess, become a Queen and restore the power of the Ennead.

A coronation and we will invite all the divine and immortals to witness you become powerful," Rene explained as Maya didn't feel so sure about it.

" A coronation, Really ! " Maya was terrified.

" You are Bastet, the goddess of protection trust me nothing wrong will happen because I will make sure of it," Rene assured Maya who was surprisingly scared and trusted her sister.

Maya went to her room to read more when she heard a prayer from Seth and she refused him.

Seth was trying to contact her.

"Bastet come on, listen to my prayer I got something important to tell you," Seth called out to her and nothing.

"She's not listening to your prayer is she ?" Emmy laughed.

"Maybe you can pray to her !" Seth asked her and she rolled her eyes.

"Over my dead body," Emmy answered him as they where back in Egypt in a Sha camp.

Bastet could see everything from the Aaru the field of reeds the home of the Egyptian gods.

Bastet eyes could see into the mortal real.

Her green cat eyes could see her father planning a strategy against the Sha with the Lynx council.

Her eyes could also see her Mother at her model agency.

But there was one he couldn't find.

She couldn't see Ivan.

"Where was he ?" she thought.

Back in the mortal realm Seth had a letter sent to Mayas father.

"A letter came in for you," Lyla came into the office and handed over the letter.

"Thank you," Connor thanked his wife as he opened the letter to see it was from Seth.

He wanted them to meet.

For a Sha and Lynx truce.

"Is he crazy ?" Connor thought as he showed Lyla who couldn't help but chuckle.

"It's an obvious ambush, he's wants blood and we will give it to him," Connor said to his wife.

"He wants us to meet up today at midnight," Lyla questioned.

" It's a good thing we see in the dark and now Bastet grows powerful and so do we, " Connor was confident of what was to happened he would win.

Maya went to Thoth the lord of wisdom and knowledge to ask him.

" I can't see him anywhere ? " She asked.

" You are still mortal and your goddess half hasn't fully manifested. It might be to much for you to use the sight," Thoth explained.

" No it's not my power, I really can't find him and am going," Maya revealed as Thoth stopped her.

" That would be unwise," Thoth pleaded.

" I got seven lives left, I'll be okay." Maya said to him as he added they should go together.

They returned to the mortal realm right in Metro City the last place she saw him in and they went to his apartment.

" Humanity has come a long way from caves to pyramids and now skyscrapers." Thoth made an observation as Maya laughed.

" I should show you the internet," Maya suggested.

" Before the internet there was me,

I will always be the original, the mortals would pray to me for wisdom and I would grant it to them," Thoth said to Maya as they took the elevator to Ivan's floor.

" So much has changed," Maya thought as she herself was a god and would stay the same as people will change as everything as well changes.

" The journey of a god is many things and sometimes we get forgotten along the way and the mortals die and go get reincarnated or spend their after life in the Aaru or the Duat if they are naughty." Thoth explained as they arrived on the floor and they stepped out of the elevator and went to find Ivan's apartment door open as Maya could smell dog.

" Ivan, " she ran in to find three men inside who were tearing up the place and immediately their eyes crossed with Maya they turned and Mayas turned green.

" Sha, " Maya whispered as Thoth had his ankh appear.

" It was Seth who sent you here, where is ivan ? " Maya asked as they knew who she was.

" Listen we don't want any problems with gods, Seth sent us to find him." One of the three men explained as Maya yelled out liar as she went at them and they fought back and it was a full on fight.

" Your going to die Sha, " Thoth laughed as he threw one of the men with his finger through a wall.

Maya grabbed the man who talked.

" Tell me everything," She said to him as the third guy tore a gas pipe in the wall and threw a lighter at it as Maya saw them and the man slipped through her hands and they grabbed their friend on the floor and they jumped out the window as Maya took Thoth to run to safety but he didn't move.

" We are gods maya, fire is nothing to us," Thoth spoke as the apparent blew up but then it didn't as Thoth held his ankh as the fire was all around them but didn't burn them as he used his ankh to absorb the fire into the ankh itself.

The ankh disappeared and he clapped his hand restoring the apartment to how it was before.

" That's a cool trick," Maya said to Thoth as he went to the window and looked out to see the men already gone.

" They are gone," He told Maya.

" It's fine, let them go I found what I was looking for and you wouldn't believe what he just told me ," Maya tells Thoth.

" What did he say ? "

" He said they are looking for Ivan because he is Shezmu," Maya tells Thoth who wasn't shocked or surprised.

" I've been very wary of him, we stripped him of his powers and he was left as an immortal to roam the earth. He must have found a new power source cause his scent and aura was on you the day we met," Thoth explained.

" I only hang around my friends and family," Maya tells him .

" He's a shape shifter and he never had an animal form cause he loved the mortal form more, and that's why we have to find Ivan cause if he is Shezmu then we are all in grave danger," Thoth explained as Maya had her brothers calling her and she focused on her brothers.

" Bastet our father is in danger. He went to meet up with Seth and go to war," Omar said her.

" Come Maya and stop this before anyone gets hurt. " Cairo prayed as Maya turned to Thoth.

" I have to go to Egypt," Maya says to Thoth with full panic.

The war of the Sha and Lynx was about to begin.

Chapter 17

Under the light of the moon, the Sha and Lynx met in the desert.

"We came here for peace," Seth said to Connor as each force stood between a line.

Seth had is Sha with him and Emmy tagged alone.

"Emmy what are you doing with him ?" Connor asked as Emmys eyes turned to that of a Sha.

"Mr Amun, we are not what you think and as much as I hate to admit this we are not the bad guys and Seth is not evil, it's Ivan he is the evil one and he killed Lucia.

He is Shezmu and you have to believe me," Emmy explained as Connor didn't believe them.

"You are now one of them, you are brainwashed and you will face the same consequences as them," Connor said to Emmy.

"Listen to me, all the hate you feel shouldn't be pointed to us but to Ivan," Seth spoke.

"The Sha is ready for peace and the you should agree to this truce. We come in peace," Emmy explained as Connor had his men pull out their arms and gunfire and the Sha did as well.

"Everyone call down," Seth tried to calm both sides.

"You are a lair and manipulative, After all you are a dog and we are Lynx,"Connor laughed as the Sha got triggered and both sides began to attack each other.

An all out battle under the moonlight.

"You are mine,"Connor pointed at Seth going after him and punching him.

"That hurt,"Seth couldn't believe it.

"The lynx are stronger,"Connor spoke with his eyes that of vengeance.

Seth couldn't believe it.

Connor managed to shoot Seth three times and pulled out his dagger and stabbed Seth right in his hand as he tried to defend himself.

"you can heal but the pain that is what I want to last,"Connor spoke as he went on with the attack.

It was a brutal fight and the lynx where winning.

Maya arrived to the blood shed and fighting.

"No," She cried out as her roar echoed the entire desert as everyone stopped and looked up to see Maya as she took a big jump landing in the middle of the battle ground.

"What are you doing to each other, what is this," Maya asked as she looked around seeing men and women hurt and others on the ground.

"You are all the children of the great Ennead, we are almost going extinct and yet here you are killing each other like a bunch of wild animals," Maya spoke as she saw a female Sha warrior on the ground and helped her up.

Everyone couldn't believe it.

"We should stop this endless violence at once," Maya spoke as she saw the female Sha warrior was injured and Maya placed her hand on the woman's forehead and healed her.

Unlocking new powers in the process.

Maya looked around and saw most injured and unleashed a wave of healing on to the crowd healing everyone including Seth.

"Our differences are many that is true,

we are different but something that we share is we are connected to something bigger.

we are unique beings.

We are night creatures, heck we share the moon. Suddenly our differences are the same." Maya said to them.

"Daughter what do you mean ?

They are our enemies since the beginning of time, he killed you. "Connor said to Maya.

"But yet am still here, it's time for forgiveness and unity," Maya said with a chuckle.

"now I understand why Ra gave me another chance it just wasn't for me to live again but to unite us as one people again, no more violence against each other or prejudice, we are one." Maya looked around seeing everyone smiling and the Sha and Lynx together in harmony for the first time in years and her heart fell full.

She began to glow and fly above as everyone looked to her.

The other Egyptian gods felt it as well.

Even Shezmu.

Maya had fully come into her full god powers and she transformed into as Seth couldn't believe it as he took transformed and his full god powers returned.

Maya returned to the ground and she had changed and turned to see Seth was changed too.

The Lynx and Sha bowed to them both.

Seth couldn't understand.

"Ra's punishment only afflicts those who are truly guilty and it looks like Ra has given not only me a second chance but you as well," Maya explains to Seth.

"Long Live Bastet," Connor spoke as Maya told them to rise up as Maya hugged her father.

"Look what you did, you united us," Connor whispered to Maya.

"Am so proud of you but how did you know ?" Connor asked.

"Two brave Lynx boys told me what would be happening," Maya told her father as Seth and Emmy came closer to them.

"Your little boyfriend is Shezmu," Emmy broke the news.

"Unfortunately it's true, I was in his apartment with Thoth and he used mirror magic and we saw every move that he took and we saw him transform," Maya revealed as Connor couldn't believe it.

"We have to find him, he must answer for what he has done, he killed you and framed me and planted memories of me killing you and I actually believed it and Ra's punishment turned me into stone for hundreds of years," Seth explained as Maya agreed.

"He has alot to pay for and finding him is our first priority," Maya added.

"No it's your coronation, it's time for the great Enneads power to be restored and for you to seat on Ra's Throne," Rene spoke as she and the rest of the Ennead had arrived.

Connor couldn't believe his eyes.

"Sobek the lord of rebirth,

Thoth the lord of wisdom,

Khepri the lord of the winds

Khnun the lord of the Earth

And Renenutet the goddess of love,

You are all here," Connor couldn't believe it.

" Great they are all here," Seth rolled his eyes.

" You are one to talk," Rene questioned back.

" If you haven't heard am innocent and my banishment is over and believe me am taking my seat in the Aaru and after Bastet's coronation we hunt Shezmu," Seth replied back as Rene smiled and Maya joined the rest of the gods and turned around to look at Seth.

" Come on let's go home," Maya said to him as he joined them and together they shot into the sky leaving the Sha and Lynx standing there watching.

" What do we do now ? " Emmy asked.

" We go find Shezmu for Seth and Bastet," Connor answered and it was a new dawn for the shifters.

Meanwhile Shezmu was in New York and he was waiting for Sophie Hill to return from work.

" Ivan you scared me, how did you get in ? " Sophie asked.

" Doesn't matter," he answered as he began to transform into his strange looking self.

His true Shezmu form.

" I didn't want it to get this dirty but she demand this of me," Ivan explained to her as he didn't want to do any of it.

" Ivan who ? " Sophie asked,

" She hates your daughter and wants her dead and there is nothing I or anyone can do," Ivan explained.

" Maya is she okay ?

Tell me atleast that ! " Sophie asked him.

" She is, " he answered her that before kidnapped Maya's mother.

Chapter 18

" I 've only seven lives left. " Maya remember as she was reading about transferring her life force.

She hopped that it would never come to it as she remembered poor Lucia who died cause she was powerless then but now she wasn't.

Meanwhile Seth missed the Aaru and he was finally home.

The field of reeds, home to the Egyptian deities.

While Emmy was filled with jealousy to the thought of Seth and Maya bonding.

Which she couldn't have been more right about in her entire life.

" You've been out here for a while ? " Maya asked Seth who smiled.

" I missed this place, it lived in the memory of my mind, " he answered as Maya agreed that it was a beautiful realm that Ra made for them.

" Look at you now, " Seth says to Maya.

" What ? " Maya answered as Seth moved close to her.

" Do you now remember me and the life we had together ? " He asked.

"When I unlocked my full god half I remember everything and you couldn't have killed me or hurt me," Maya said moving closer to Seth.

She looked into his dark black eyes and he into her enchanting green eyes.

"So beautiful," he whispers.

"Shezmu is still out there and as long as he is out there we can never know peace," Maya says to Seth who made a promise to her.

"I will stop him and everything he has done to us he and whoever is involved will pay," he promised as Rene watched them through a magic orb.

"It's almost time and only one of us will ascend to our fathers throne and may the best goddess win," Rene laughed as she was getting ready to enact her plan.

Thousands of years in the making.

Connor received a message from Ryan Ustet and Ash and it wasn't good news.

"She's missing ?" Connor asked,

"No taken, It was Ivan." Ryan stated walking around Sophie's apartment.

"I got a scent and am pursuing alone," Ryan stated as Connor agreed and he was taking a flight out of Egypt to New York.

"Both the Sha and Lynx are coming with me cause it's about damn time we end this," Connor spoke through the phone.

Back in the Aaru the day of Bastet's Coronation had arrived and she was about to fulfill a long standing prophecy and she was about to restore the power of the Great Ennead and finally destroy Apophis, also known as Apep, an ancient Egyptian deity associated with chaos, darkness, and destruction.

The day was here and Bastet was thrilled and finally ready unlike the first time.

Maya looked at the mirror and herself and couldn't believe the timid young model who obeyed her mother and didn't have a voice was now Bastet the goddess of protection and soon the goddess of creation.

She couldn't help but smile.

" Good thing you are here Bastet," Rene came in with bad news.

" Renenutet what's wrong ? " Maya asked.

" It's your mother, Shezmu has her but she is okay and I know where she is," Rene explained.

" How ? " Maya asked,

" Am the goddess of love," Rene explained taking Maya's hand.

" Let's go save her," Rene said to Maya who agreed.

" Let's get the rest of the Ennead and together we can stop him," Maya asked her sister.

" You are now a full on god and am the goddess of love we can definitely stop an ex god like Shezmu, he won't see us coming, " Rene reminded Maya as they left to the mortal realm and Seth came in and found them gone.

Shezmu had Sophie with him in an abandoned fish dock.

He didn't tie up and she was trying to talk to him and he told her he had orders.

" From who ? " Sophie asked,

" I can't tell you more but know one thing I won't hurt you and everything will be okay that's if Bastet will be able to do it," Shezmu said to her as Rene punched him throwing him across the fish dock.

" Maya ! " Sophie cried out as Maya ran to her mother.

" Are you okay ? " Maya asked her mother.

" Am okay and woah you look incredible? " Sophie said to her daughter.

" He's getting up," Rene called to attention.

As Maya moved Infront of her mother.

" Ivan ?

So it's really you," Maya couldn't believe it.

" Well I didn't want it to be this way but I have no choice," Shezmu said to Maya.

" I loved you! " Maya whispered.

" I still love you and no one or anything will ever make me feel otherwise, believe me I came to care for you and I will never forgive myself for hurting you," Shezmu spoke as Ivan as Maya felt tears fall down her face for Shezmu as Rene began attacking him with lighting bolts and Maya couldn't move as she remembered all the good times she had with Ivan.

" Bastet do something, " Rene called out as Maya screamed throwing an even bigger bolt of lightning at Shezmu who managed to dodge and threw daggers at them as Rene took Bastet's hand and together they made a pyramid shield over them to protect them from the daggers.

Sophie moved back and stepped out of the shield as a dagger came at her and Rene saw and moved Infront of Sophie and the dagger hit her stabbing her very hard as she fell to the ground and Maya dropped the shield running to her sister.

" Renenutet! " Maya held her.

" Why aren't you healing ? " Maya asked.

" Because he's shezmu," Rene whispered as she was dying.

" Poor Bastet the only one who believed in you is going to die again. It's not like you can save her," Shezmu scoffed.

Maya remember she can transfer one of her lives to another and she pulled out the dagger and placed her hand on Rene's head.

" I am BASTET, goddess of protection and heir to Ra and I bestow one of my lives to you Goddess of Love, breathe, live again," Maya called out as she felt a part of her leave and one of her lives went into Rene who opened her eyes and the wound immediately healed.

Renenutet immediately got on her feet and she could feel the life force of Bastet flowing with in her as both Bastet and Sophie looked at her.

Rene couldn't help but laugh as Shezmu bowed.

" I have earned my freedom," Shezmu asked as Rene turned around and blew her hand and pink dust was released and when Sophie breathed it in she fell to the floor.

" Mom," Maya screamed as she used her powers to help her mother not hit the ground hard but delicately.

" She's just a sleep Bastet," Rene explained as she turned to look at Shezmu and she gave him his freedom.

" You did well, " Rene said to Shezmu as Maya couldn't under-stand.

" Am sure you are wondering what is happening it's your sister that's who and she hates you more than anything,

it's always been her.

I've just been a slave to her." Shezmu explained as he made two swords appear and in her hands.

" Who I will kill if it's the last thing i do, " Shezmu said aloud as Rene laughed.

" Definitely the last thing, " Rene blew at her hand at him and this wasn't pink dust but blue smoke and it froze him and he couldn't move.

" You dare threaten your new Queen, " Rene asked as she burnt him alive with her mind as he screamed in agony and Maya couldn't believe it.

Rene then made the ground open and swallow Shezmu as Rene laughed turning to her sister Bastet.

" Shezmu was evil but to kill you was never one of his plans because why would he want you ?

Because I wanted you and I waited for you for centuries and the first time I wanted an easy death for you but now I see death is too good for you, because you keep coming back like the roach you are ? " Rene screamed.

" We are sisters ? " Maya asked her.

" Am not your sister, infact since you first appeared I hated you,

Bastet is more beautiful, powerful, intelligent, it was always you and I lived with it but when our father choose you over me to be his successor he made me the laughing stock of our pantheon.

I was the first born, his throne is suppose to be mine and not you and that made you my enemy, " Rene began walking towards Maya who used her power to send her mother back to her apartment.

" It's time for Rene to win , " Rene opened a doorway and kicked Maya into it as it closed.

"Say hello to the old man," she whispered before returning to the Aaru and finding everything ready.

" Great let's get on with it ! " Rene announced as everyone asked where Bastet was ?.

" Shezmu had kidnapped Bastet's mortal mother and she went to save her but was killed by Shezmu,

Luckily I was able to have followed and managed to kill him and I saved her but before he killed her seven times right before me and now she's gone to be with Ra," Rene cried as Seth could clearly see her tears where faked.

" Before she left this realm she made me her successor, " Rene revealed shocking the other gods.

" I don't think it's that easy," Seth laughed as the others did laugh and went to Ra's Throne and took a seat and nothing happened to her as Ra's power began to flow within her as they all finally believed her.

" Bastet," Seth couldn't believe it as the great Ennead all took a bow to their new Queen who's first act was to restore the powers of the great Ennead.

Seth remember what Shezmu said he was and that was a slave and he looked to Rene who was transformed and now primordial.

He remembered she was the goddess of love and one of her powers was to enslave men.

He knew something terrible had happened to Bastet.

Sophie woke up in her bed and went to her living room to find Emmy, Ash, Ryan and Connor there and they where surprised.

Sophie told them what had happened and right as she finished explained all the Lynx in the room began to feel something strange.

" What is it ? " Ash asked Ryan.

" I've lost all my power," He answered as Connor to and his men as well.

His phone began to ring and he answered and it was the same report as Lynx all around the world where loosing their powers.

"What does this mean ?" Sophie asked.

"That Bastet isn't alive anymore," Connor answered dropping to his knees as Sophie burst out into tears.

Little did they know that she was still alive and Rene had sent her to a prison world where her powers didn't work and the prison world was an endless desert.

There was Maya trapped and didn't have a way back home since her powers didn't work.

But right as she was giving up she found new hope.

"Bastet !" Someone familiar called out as Maya looked to see it was him.

"I must be hallucinating it can't be you," Maya said to herself as he approached her and hugged her.

"Great Osiris it's you my daughter," He said to her.

"Ra it's really you father," Maya couldn't believe it as he was right Infront of her.

"Let me guess Renenutet," Ra asked.

"Yes how did you know ?" Maya was surprised.

"She sent me here a millennia ago," Ra answered.

"So we are not dead?

Because you are dead !

This is not some kind of an afterlife?" Maya asked.

"We are both much still very alive and not dead," Ra said to Maya.

"How do we go back to stop her?" Maya asked.

"There is no way out and we are better off trapped her cause Renenutet is sinister and her evil plans are only just beginning and we are better off being here than out there with her," Ra explained as he began to walk off and maya followed him as all she could see was just sand and nothing else.

Chapter 19

S eth went to Earth to find out what he heard was indeed the truth.

She was really gone and yet he didn't believe it in his heart.

The Lynx had lost their strength.

Seth knew it was all Rene's fault.

" She's gone and even if I wasn't one of her biggest fans I didn't want her to die," Emmy confessed to Seth.

" I don't believe it, my heart tells me she's alive and she's out there, somewhere! " Seth revealed as he disappeared and went to see Sophie.

" How are you ? " Seth asked.

" Terrible, my only daughter has died, " Sophie sarcastically answered.

" I know but she would want you to be strong, I will bring her back, " Seth said you her as she took his hand and confessed.

" My heart doesn't believe she is dead, " Sophie told him.

" A mother knows and I know she is not dead but that Rene did something, I don't know what but she did, " Sophie explained to Seth who believed her and knew something was going on.

" I will do all in my power to bring Bastet, I mean Maya home back to you, " Seth promised as he returned to the Aaru to face Rene.

" You did something,

I don't know what but I know you did, " Seth faced Rene who sat on Ra's Throne as she laughed.

" She was my sister, I loved her and I did everything to make sure she grew powerful and I supported her, besides if I did something to her why would I be next in line ? " Rene asked,

Seth was confused and had nothing to say as he took a bow and left the throne room and was met by Khepri who took him to his room.

" Khepri if this is what I think it is then am not in the mood, " Seth complained.

" No it's not what you think, it's about Bastet, " khepri revealed.

" What do you know ? " Seth urged him to reveal.

" I have spies all over the place, " Khepri revealed as he had a scarab on his hand and it showed footage in a hologram form and it was Bastet in her room with Rene who was convincing her to go but Bastet wanted to get the help of the Ennead.

" I knew it was her," Seth watched the footage as Rene and Bastet left and the scarab scanned the room and found a book about life transfer.

" What does this mean ? " Seth asked as khepri had the book in his hand.

" It means Bastet transferred one of her lives to Rene that explains why she can sit on that throne cause Bastet didn't crown her before she died. That's if she even died," Khepri explained as Seth knew he had to go to the underworld.

" Keep Scarab next to you, as a way of communicating," Khepri said to Seth who agreed as he travelled to the Underworld.

Seth arrived at the Duat the underworld to find Bastet cause she was half mortal and maybe there was a chance he would see her again there.

He was met by Ma'at the goddess, personification of truth, cosmic balance, and justice. Her ostrich feather represents the truth.

While other gods have Ankhs Ma'at had a Feather and all living things would pass her for judgment and your heart was weighed against her feather.

If your heart was light as her feather you would go to the Aaru and find peace but it your heart was heavy than her feather then you would be sent to eternal damnation in the pits of fire.

" Ma'at goddess of judgment and justice I have come to you for help, I need to find Bastet." Seth explained.

" Bastet the goddess of life and protection, half goddess and half mortal I know of her and heard stories of her," Ma'at knew everything.

" Have you seen her ? " Seth asked.

" She isn't dead cause I see every mortal life from beginning to their end and her end hasn't happened yet, " Ma'at explained to Seth who was surprised.

" The lynx have lost their powers and she isn't in the Aaru or in the mortal realm, " Seth explained as Ma'at laughed.

" We both know that there are prison world and before we used to banish and stripe away powers we would throw the worst of the worst in prison worlds where their powers and nature would not work at all.

It was like death of some sort, " Ma'at reminded Seth.

Seth finally knew everything as he put in place everything.

He went to face Rene with the entire Ennead present.

" You enslaved Shezmu and made him kill Bastet centuries ago and then again but this time you didn't just kill her but you sent her to a prison world," Seth exposed Rene who laughed.

" You have me figured out don't you, before Ra ruled he over-threw Osiris and before Zeus ruled he overthrew the titans.

It's what we do,

Besides you and this entire Ennead know that I was to be my father's successor and yet you never back me up when my father threw me to the side to play favourites with Bastet,

I was his first born and yet am last,

No way in hell," Rene stood up as she held on to the staff of Ra.

" If you love her so much then go join her," Rene screamed as she opened a doorway and threw Seth in before closing it.

Turning to the Ennead.

" Things are going to change around here, first off am not going to hide anything and you all better bend the knee to me or die.

It's that simple," Rene hit her staff on the floor as it echoed through the entire throne room as the gods bend the knee.

" Good, now Thoth am going to need your help with something, " Rene asked him.

As both Khepri, sobek and Khnum looked to Thoth.

" What is it ? " He asked.

" I want us to completely free Apep and I want to control it and become the most powerful god in existence." Rene laughed.

" You want to free Apophis the eater ?

It is an animal without reason or emotion, it will be the end of us and kill us all." Sobek tried to reason with Rene.

" That's why I want to control it, I am want to erase all the mortals and create a new utopia where we will be worshiped and not technology or money.

A world for us to reshape and make into whatever we want, " Rene explained her plans to them as they couldn't believe it.

She was out of control and they where all in danger.

Seth woke up in a desert and it was night time already and as he got up he saw Ra standing a few meters from him with Bastet there as she couldn't believe it.

" Bastet, " Seth whispered as she ran to him hugging him.

" You found me," Bastet said to him.

" I always do." Seth answered.

Chapter 20

The desert is a hot and unforgiving place not for the weak, Seth's home ever since Ra found him as a baby in the deserts.

Ra knew he wasn't an ordinary child and so he took him and named him Seth the lord of the desert storms.

Seth couldn't believe it.

Both Bastet and Ra where alive and Infront of him.

" How is this possible ? " Seth asked looking at Ra.

" I know we all thought he was dead but he's been here, Rene trapped him here all this time! " Maya explained as Ra went Infront of Seth and extended his hand.

Seth took it and was pulled into a hug by Ra.

" Set am sorry for all I have done to you," Ra said to him.

" You where my weapon, my desert storm. I should have know better that it was the lies of Rene," Ra repented.

" You did what you thought you had to do and I would have done the same cause Bastet is the love of both our existence," Seth explained as he and Ra looked at Bastet who smiled.

" If you both loved me then you should help me get out of here so I can finally have that pending conversation with my sister, " Bastet asked.

" There is no way out of here and we can't communicate with anyone outside of this prison ! " Ra explained to Seth who took the scarab from his pocket.

" Is that what I think it is ? " Ra knew it.

" A scarab courtesy of Khepri, " Seth explained as he called to Khepri who heard the call and answered it.

" Seth, " Khepri called out.

" Am still alive and am here with Bastet and you won't believe who else Ra, " Seth revealed as Khepri couldn't believe it.

" He died ? " khepri answered.

" For the god of the air and skies you sure don't have faith and yet you have wings that fly, " Ra spoke to him and he couldn't believe it.

" Ra it's really you my king, " Khepri was excited as he told them Rene's plans.

" she wants to free Apep and destroy all the mortals, she's crazy and drunk on power," Khepri explained as Bastet knew she had to get out now more than ever.

" We will need the god of wisdoms help? " Seth asked and Khepri went to Thoth immediately and told him.

" It's an unfinished world so there has to be a failsafe Incase she wanted to take out anyone she sent there, " Thoth revealed as Maya, Seth and Ra heard him.

" I've tried everything and I can't find it, " Ra explained.

" Well it's a world made of sand so the door to escape that realm must be in it." Thoth explained as Seth looked around.

" You are Seth, lord of the desert.

This realm may be a prison but it's still your domain," Ra spoke to Seth who wasn't sure about it.

"Feel each grain of sand and feel the Earth underneath and then find that door," Ra said to him as Bastet and Ra gave him room.

Seth began to concentrate and he said could feel everything as he began to move the sand and he could feel the door.

"It obeys you not the other way around," Ra yelled as Seth parted the sand and moved the desert and the earth beneath them.

Maya couldn't believe it.

It was incredible.

Moving them to their way out.

Seth finally took his breath and couldn't believe what he had just done.

"Did I

really do that," He asked out of breath.

"Yes you did cause you are a god and there is nothing a god can't do, our limit doesn't exist and we keep evolving," Ra answered as he also turned to look at Maya.

"Let's go home," Maya said to them as they ran out of that prison world and immediately it got destroyed and Rene could feel it.

"They escaped," She screamed as her fury and rage was elevated.

But Rene didn't have time for that cause she was about to tame Apep.

"They will regret leaving that prison world," Rene made a promise.

Seth, Maya and Ra where back in the mortal Realm in a of grain in Egypt.

"You did it,

We couldn't have escaped if it wasn't for you," Maya hugged Seth as Ra agreed.

The return of the Bastet the Lynx began to regain their power and they could feel her again.

"The connection is back," Connor gasped as Omar and Cairo ran out calling him and he followed them and found the Lynx and Sha there in a large crowd and he went closer and he could see her.

Maya was hugging her brothers as she spotted her father.

"Maya," Connor couldn't believe it as he ran to hug her and she ran to him.

They hugged tightly.

"I was scared you where gone forever," Connor breathed.

"I was gone to," Seth joked as they all laughed.

"If there is someone here who knows the pain you feel from loosing Bastet it's me," Ra revealed to Connor.

Connor was confused by who he was.

"Father this is Ra," Maya explained as everyone heard and they all went on their knees.

"Lord Ra," Connor couldn't believe it.

"Is that him the OG of the gods ?" Cairo asked his older brother who pulled him down.

"You may all rise," Ra said to them.

"I am just Ramunet but am no longer a god so just call me Ra," Ra explained to them as Connor couldn't believe it as he was hugged by Ra.

"You raised a brave, strong daughter twice over again am sure no easy task," Ra spoke to Connor who couldn't take any credit.

"She's here," Seth whispered to Maya as he pointed to a taxi that was heading towards the Maya's father's home.

The taxi door opened and it was Sophie.

" Mom," Maya whispered as her mother smiled to see her daughters beautiful face again as they ran and embraced.

" You are here," Sophie asked.

" Am here and no one is going to separate you from me ever again. I love you mom," Maya promised her mother.

As Rene back in the Aaru watched with the other gods who deep down where happy that bastet was back.

" Time for the war to begin," Rene announced as she went to he balcony and used the powers of Ra to free Apep from the spell and boundary that kept him trapped and it was once again free to eat all of creation.

But something went wrong with Apophis and he broke himself free.

Chapter 21

Bastet was happy to be home and sad for a war was about to happen.

The Ennead was about to go to war.

"Thank you for helping us get out of there ! " Maya tells Seth.

"I made a promise to you a long time ago to protect you from everything including myself," Seth revealed to Maya looking into her green emerald eyes.

"Your eyes are beautiful, just like looking at them for the first time," Seth whispered as he moved closer and she moved closer when they heard two throats clear.

"That would be my two father," Maya smiled as she and Seth looked and saw both Ra and Connor standing a distance away from them.

They had not left Egypt and were still at Connors home at the lynx compound.

Seth extended his hand to Maya who took it and they held hands and joined the rest of their family.

"A war is coming ! " Ra spoke to them as they all gathered around the fire under the full moon.

"Not just a war for the gods but a war for the lynx and the Sha," Ra explained as Seth and Maya looked to each other.

"To late the war is already here," Rene voice echoed as a bright light brought not just her but the rest of the Ennead.

"The end of the world is here," Thoth the lord of wisdom announced.

"Don't tell me!" Ra knew only one thing could be happening.

"she released Apophis in an attempt to control him but then he went crazy and he is consuming the Aaru as we speak and next up the underworld before this realm and all of existence," Thoth broke the bad news.

"You stupid child,

You thought you could control Apophis !" Ra laughed at Re-nenutet.

"It's a world eater, an animal without a conscious , ruthless without a mind and you can't control something without a mind.

Thought the goddess of love would know that," Ra yelled at Rene who had fear of her father as it was evident in her eyes and Maya could see it.

"The only way to kill Apophis is to complete the prophecy and my successor will have that power," Ra spoke as Maya looked at him.

"Give me that," Ra spoke as he took back his staff and all his power back from Rene turning her back to the goddess of love.

"Bastet vs Rene will face off in a series of challenge to see it they are worthy to be my successor and Queen." Ra spoke as he raised his staff looking at his daughters.

"Bastet,

Be careful," Seth whispered as Maya hugged him going to Ra.

Rene couldn't believe it Ra was giving her chance to prove herself.

"We don't have much time," Ra said to the two of them as Rene and Bastet both held the staff and it turned to sand along with them and they where off to go face the challenge of Ra.

"My the best goddess win," Seth whispered as they all watched Rene and Bastet go.

Chapter 22

The Field of Reeds aka reincarnation place known as Aaru and Duat the underworld.

Bastet and Rene arrived at the beginning of time and the civilization of Egypt.

To find two kids playing.

"Where are we ? " Rene thought as she went to ask the three kids.

Only to find Bastet there asking one of the kids and she decided to ask the other one.

"Small child where am I ?" Rene asked as Bastet laughed.

"No need they can't see or hear us," Bastet answered as Rene rolled her eyes.

"Aaru, Duat," a woman called out as Rene couldn't believe it.

"The two," Rene couldn't believe it.

"Their sacrifice turns them into legends and created new realms or existence, the underworld, the afterlife, " Bastet wondered by they where there.

"Their story is a cautionary tale on kindness to those who die, humility to those who end up in the afterlife. That life and death are one," Rene remembered.

"That's beautifully spoken,

But why would Ra want us to learn this ?" Bastet wondered.

"Good question, why would he want us to learn this, " Rene thought.

The two sisters sat on two rocks and watched as the two little girls played.

"I don't actually hate you, what I hate is that our father picks you over me," Rene revealed as Bastet knew what she was talking about.

"But don't you see our father Wanted you here and believes in you ," Bastet said to Rene who smiled and went in for a hug and Bastet couldn't believe it also going in for the hug only to get stabbed by Rene.

A fatal, life ending stab.

"Sorry sis now you only got five lives," Rene whispered blowing a kiss at her baby her sister as Bastet eyes closed and she died.

Only to return back to life waking up on a roof top.

"That little snake," Bastet thought as she looked to see where she was only to discover she was back in Egypt.

Using her enhanced vision she could spot Rene flying across the city.

Looking ahead to see a large orb of power literally across the city and Rene was heading there.

"Ra's power," Bastet panicked as she jumped of that building taking to skies after Rene.

Behind Rene.

"I can't believe you killed me, " Bastet screamed.

"Technically I didn't you still have five lives left," Rene laughed as she was in the lead.

Bastet stopped when she noticed a big fire and immediately went to check what was happening to find a mother and a young boy trapped in the building and went inside.

"Don't worry I will get you out," Bastet told them as she raised her hand and her Ankh appeared and a protection shield appeared around the mother and her son transporting them out of the building.

Taking them outside as Bastet saw the fire department arrive to end the fire as she looked and saw Rene get the power and transform.

"She did it," Bastet smiled as the woman came and hugged Bastet thanking her for saving them.

"You are one of a kind," She said to Bastet as she and her son walked away.

Rene came down flying.

"You did it," Bastet congratulated Rene who didn't feel all powerful.

"I don't feel extremely powerful," Rene explained as Bastet didn't understand why.

"You clearly won," Bastet thought.

"no she didn't ," Ra spoke as he appeared and everything around them changed as they stood in the desert.

"You don't feel the power because you failed," Ra broke the news to Rene.

"If I didn't win then who did ?

She !

But she did nothing," Rene yelled.

"Bastet passes the test cause she saved that mother and son in the burning building," Ra turned to Bastet.

" I didn't catch the orb of power, " Bastet defended.

" This whole test was to tech you about balance of life and death.

It's why the test begins in the first age with Aaru and Duat as children, who played together before they became the After life and the underworld.

Two different entities yet they coexist together working for the same purpose, " Ra explained as Rene couldn't believe it.

" Do you know why we the Ennead reign over the desert ? " Ra asked Bastet who never thought of that question before.

" Why father ? " Bastet asked,

" It's because we grow in the most harshest environment, we get stronger under the burning sun with our bare feet on the hot sand.

Because we are strong and we can endure everything, " Ra spoke to Bastet and Rene.

Ra took both his daughters hands.

Placing them together.

" We are family and it's time we learn to forgive each other and we become one," Ra said to them.

" The final battle is near as Apophis nears," Ra tried to connect them together.

" I won and the power is mine, " Rene confessed as Bastet turned to look at her in shock.

" You clearly have no respect for life nor have love in your heart, and so I strip away your immortality and all your power, I have tried to look away and protect you and let it go.

You once were going to be my successor but then I saw through your heart and I choose Bastet and now after everything you have done I see you are not deserving to even be a goddess and so I strip your birthright," Ra punished Rene as she couldn't believe it as she cried and called out to her father and Bastet.

" my king, my pharaoh, punish her but don't let let suffer," Bastet begged of Ra and he accepted.

" Even after all she has done you still have compassion, I have listened to you my Bastet and the goddess of love will become mortal and she will live among them and will be safe and no harm will come to you.

You will have my protection but not from old age and sickness and so I banish you forever," Ra spoke as he took her ankh and it turned to sand in his hands.

Rene began to loose all her powers and her goddess look began to fade as she cried out to her father and Sister but they just watched as she was taken away by a sand storm.

" Thank you father for sparing her ," Bastet thanked Ra as told her it was time and he bestowed his power upon her and she was now the goddess of life and protection.

" He is almost here now go stop him, you are ready and your entire life has led you here.

This is your destiny, " Ra praised Bastet as the great Ennead appeared all around Bastet with their Ankhs floating Infront of them as they channelled their power into their ankhs and thought it to Bastet.

Making her extremely powerful as she took to the skies and went to the realm in between the Aaru and the mortal Realm.

Only to be met by a darkness that was unlike any other.

" Bastet the goddess of protection we meet again, " Apophis spoke to her as it showed it's terrifying face to Bastet.

Chapter 23

Long Ago Ra was the solar deity, bringer of light, and thus the upholder of all that was good while Apep / Apophis was as the greatest enemy of Ra, and thus was given the title Enemy of Ra, and also "the god of Chaos".

Apophis eater of light and to some he was a titan who couldn't be defeated by Ra but by his kin.

" Meet Again ? " Bastet answered the creature.

" Your essence was used to hold me back and contain me all these centuries, don't you remember? " Apophis asked.

" Banishing of Chaos, " Bastet remember.

" But now you have changed young goddess, you aren't the god I last faced, " Apophis whispered.

" I faced off with you and my father and the Ennead was also there, " Bastet remember how they managed to contain him.

The great Ennead combined all their power and Bastet being the goddess of protection was the final ingredient.

" I know I can't kill you," Bastet said to the creature.

"Just like there is life there must also be death and I am balance, everything your father has built I will devour because you can't stop me again.

The great Ennead is over,

How many are left ?

I can the shift in the cosmos,

You aren't powerful alone to stop me," Apophis assured Bastet.

" No I will stop you, "

" How will you stop when you are human full of weaknesses, " Apophis laughed.

Bastet was getting engulfed by darkness.

It was clear Apep was stronger and the darkness was unlike anything and it was engulfing her and she felt alone and cold and scared.

" Give in to the darkness, goddess of protection.

No one can save you,

Not the Ennead or Ra.

Your are all alone, destined to stop me when you couldn't even save yourself from death when your the goddess of life, " voices began to whisper in Bastet's ears as she shed a tear and gave in as Apophis began to spread his darkness of destruction and it arrived on Earth.

Ra who stood outside looked up and saw Apophis moving .

" Bastet! " Ra whispered as Seth and the other Ennead could feel what was happening to Bastet.

" What can we do ? " Connor asked Ra.

" Pray to her and give her strength," Ra whispered as Connor sent the message out to the Lynx clan and Seth to the Sha clan.

The rest of the Ennead joined in.

" I believe in you Bastet," Seth prayed.

Bastet suddenly began to hear the voices of people who loved her, speaking to her and encouraging her in her lowest point.

She smiled and her hands began to glow and her Ankh appeared engulfing her in light as Apophis could feel the light and hope.

"Balance can always coexist and we need darkness to have light and I know what to do with you," Bastet raised her ankh and began absorbing the creature into it.

Bastet returned home to be met by a celebration.

"You did it!" Seth said hugging her as she was happy to see him and all of them.

"Your words gave me strength," Bastet revealed.

"What did you do to Apep ?" Ra asked,

"I took care of him and let's just say he won't be a problem," Bastet spoke as held her golden Ankh in her hands as Apophis cursed out Bastet and the Ennead but no one could hear him as she smiled.

Meanwhile Shezmu had returned and he was very much not dead,

The goddess of love had trapped him in a prison separate from where he had Bastet.

Now with the power of the goddess of love stripped away and there was no goddess of love he was free.

And he wanted Revenge.

It was only fair he finished what he started.

"My Beautiful Bastet if only you knew when one shadow fades away another one takes it's place," Shezmu watched Bastet as he was planning his revenge.

Chapter 24

Bastet walked through a beautiful field and found Seth standing there waiting for her.

"It's time," he whispered to her as he got close before moving aside for Bastet who looked and saw the great Ennead complete.

"All nine of us," Bastet smiled as she joined the others forming a circle and she wondered who the new gods where and she couldn't see their faces and together they where channeling power to stop a roaring Shezmu who was charging at them like a raging bull.

Bastet woke up only to find it was dream.

"Are you okay?" Seth immediately came into her room to check up on her.

"I just had a nightmare!" Bastet explained.

"I know, I saw it too." Seth revealed as Bastet got very nervous.

"I thought you don't dream?" Bastet asked.

"We don't but what you saw was a vision of our future, a prophecy that's why I saw it and am sure the rest of the remaining Ennead have seen it. Shezmu is alive." Seth said to Bastet who was just getting used to a stress free life and now she had to stop Shezmu.

"Just great," Bastet remarked as she got up from bed to go hunt for Shezmu.

Bastet and Seth returned to the Earthly plane and she went to see her father Ra.

Bastet was shocked to find the Sha and Lynx living together in the community.

"You united us and soon the Ennead," Seth said as they walked to her father's villa and she could see her brothers playing with other kids and they immediately sensed her and came running.

She was happy to see them as they run hugging her.

"You came," Cairo couldn't believe.

"I have a million questions," Omar added as Bastet smiled.

"I will always come home to you two and our father, But first I have to see my father and later I will tell you everything." Bastet said to the two.

"Well dad's in the study," Cairo pointed out.

"Not that dad but Ra," Bastet changed the question.

"He's with your mother at the fields," Omar said with a smirk as Bastet didn't understand him but Seth did as the two went to the fields.

"Wait is this a date ?" Bastet looked out and her eyes could see them.

"Look at them, they are happy," Seth said to Bastet who's eyes where cat eyes as they turned normal.

"I love your beautiful green emerald eyes," Seth whispered as Bastet looked into his eyes.

"I was so wrong about you, u are kind and selfless and I lov" Bastet was going to finish but her mother saw her and called out to her interrupting the moment.

"We will finish this conversation later," Bastet said to Seth as he laughed.

"Another pending conversation, at this point I will be waiting in a line after your brothers finally talk to you," Seth asked.

"I wouldn't have it any other way," Bastet smiled as she took his hand and they two joined her parents.

"Bastet you are here?" Ra knew there was trouble as Bastet was hugging her mother.

"It's terrible," Seth revealed as they had a seat and Bastet told him her dream.

"That's some information," Ra couldn't believe it.

"Once we returned here I could feel it, Shezmu is alive and if he is alive he surely would want revenge on me and Seth." Bastet explained.

"Maya you have us and you will not face this alone," Sophie Hill said to her daughter who was almost about to cry.

"I haven't been called Maya in a while, I think I forgot," Bastet smiled as her mother wiped her tears.

"If Shezmu is out there he will definitely go after someone he hates more than you two, someone who had him trapped in her love spell and isn't a god anymore," Ra gave the clues to Bastet and Seth and they both knew Rene was going to be the first one Shezmu will enact his vengeance on.

"She will be an easy target for him," Seth reminded them.

"I blessed her with protection and nothing can hurt her and that was courtesy of the goddess of protection, he can't kill her." Ra points out.

"But he doesn't know that and we can trap him and finally get him," Bastet smiled as she used her power of sight to search for Rene.

"I can see her, she is okay and she is in Las Vegas," Bastet closed her eyes and opened them.

"Then let's go wait for Shezmu," Seth said to Bastet who wanted him to stay.

"What about the rest of you?" Bastet wondered.

"This is a place filled with Sha and Lynx and Ra himself?" Sophie tried to calm Bastet.

"No," Bastet said to her mother.

"He knows I love you all and he might take a play this place," Bastet called for the Ennead.

"Khnum you and Seth stay behind here and protect this sanctuary,

Me, Thoth, Sobek and Khepri will go find Renenutet," Bastet gave her orders.

"I will protect them with my life," Seth gave her his word.

As she left with the rest of the Ennead to Las Vegas Nevada.

Rene arrived to her luxurious pent house removing her shoes and rubbing her feet cause of the soreness.

"Being Mortal sucks," she whispered.

"Ain't that the truth, Hotel of Love how befitting of you!" Bastet answered surprising Rene.

"Bastet, Thoth, Sobek and Khepri did you all just come here to gloat at me and couldn't even bring the whole Ennead or is my punishment over?" Rene asked with optimism.

"You wish," Thoth laughed as Bastet too laughed with the others.

"We came to protect you, Shezmu is alive and he wants revenge." Khepri explained as Rene now laughed.

"That sounds like a you problem besides why would he want to kill me?" Rene asked them.

" Did you forget you had him in your love spell and had him as your slave since forever?

Ring a bell ? " Bastet reminded her.

" Am mortal and if he wanted me dead then I would be dead days ago rotting because I was with him for a very long time and he knows this is one of my worshipers headquarters.

I've been blessing them with my presence since the stone age and he definitely knows if anything would happen to me I would come here cause this is my temple." Rene went to the small bar and fixed herself a drink as she laughed.

" This is crazy! " Bastet didn't understand.

" Am an easy prey and Shezmu doesn't love an easy prey, he's literally the hunter god of death and he has no fear in him and will do exactly what you think he won't," Rene revealed to them as Bastet began to hear people calling to her and screams.

" Let's go," Bastet could feel the pain.

" You better go there quick cause knowing Shezmu he has prob- ably slaughtered everyone you have ever know or loved," Rene's final words to Bastet as she was referring to Seth.

Bastet and the Ennead returned to the sanctuary to find a literal war zone.

Death and destruction.

" Bastet over here," Sobek called out as they went to see what it was to find a badly wounded Khnum bleeding gold.

Bastet's heart broke seeing him that way as she and the rest of the gods helped him.

" It was Shezmu he arrived immediately after you left and we tried to hold him back but he was stronger and relentless," Khnum revealed as he was breathing his lasts.

" Rest Khnum save your energy while we try get you healed, " Bastet asked of him as Thoth looked at the wound and how deep it was.

" This was shezmu's Ankh that cut you! " Thoth panicked.

" It's okay am ready," Khnum revealed to them as he began to turn into sand and returned to Earth cause he was the bull shifter and lord of the Earth.

His ankh remaining on top of the ground.

Bastet took it.

" Bastet your finally back," Ash came running .

" Where is everyone? " Bastet asked.

" Shezmu took your mother, father, Ra and Seth who he badly hurt.

Ryan and Emmy are helping evacuate the remaining Sha and Lynx out if here and the injured ones are getting help from Lyla she's with your brothers. " Ash revealed as Bastet had in hands Khepri's ankh.

" Where is Khepri? " Ash asked.

" He is gone and this is what's left of him!" Bastet revealed as Ash couldn't believe it.

" He has killed one of us again, after what he did to Lucia ." Ash had tears in his eyes.

" Lucia," Bastet thought of her and looked to Ash and she extended her hand out to Ash.

" Are you ready to do anything to avenge Lucia and help me stop Shezmu ? " Bastet asked as Ash was ready taking her hand and with the rest of the Ennead following behind.

Meanwhile Shezmu had Ra, Sophie, Connor and Seth as his prisoners and waiting for Bastet to come so they can have their final last battle.

"Let's see if you have enough lives to save them," he whispered as he sharpened his Ankh.

Epilogue

Bastet took Ash to the Aaru where she took Renenutet's Ankh and called forth for Ma'at.

As the rest of the Ennead didn't understand.

"Bastet my Queen you summon me your humble servant. I am honored," Ma'at humbly bowed before Bastet.

"I want Lucia Baker," Bastet asked.

"She is in the land of the dead, she can't return to life there must be order and I must uphold it," Ma'at defended.

"Am not saying you bring her back to life cause I will, I have six lives left.

I've seen the future Ma'at and I saw the great Ennead complete and I saw you with us," Bastet whispered to her as she asked her Ma'at for her feather and in Bastet's hand she turned it into gold and changed it into an Ankh.

Giving it to Ma'at who couldn't believe it.

"Thank you Bastet," Ma'at humbly thanked as the rest of the Ennead couldn't believe it.

"Just summon Lucia and I will do the rest," Bastet said to Ma'at who did as told and brought fourth Lucia.

"Maya, Ash." Lucia called out as she was in a ghost form.

"Am sorry it took me time but I finally got a hang of this goddess thing," Bastet extended her hand to her and Lucia took it as she began to turn corporal again.

Bastet had given her one of her lives and was left with five lives.

" I missed you," Ash hugged Lucia who hugged him back as she couldn't believe she was back.

" You are all here now," Bastet smiled.

" What's the plan like what can we do ? " Lucia asked.

" I need gods." Bastet answered as she gave Lucia the Ankh of love.

"Because you sacrificed yourself for me and died," Bastet said to Lucia.

" Because I love you," Lucia answered as the Ankh began to glow bright than it ever did as she took it and transformed into the goddess of love.

" This is for you Ash, your loyal and you have compassion and your a true friend and I couldn't trust anyone else with this power but you," Bastet handed him the Ankh which began to glow as well.

" I will do you proud ! " Ash spoke as he transformed and became the lord of the Earth.

" We have to go stop Shezmu he is the ninth member of this Ennead and we have to separate him with his Ankh. " Bastet revealed to them as they formed a circle and with their combined power they found Shezmu.

Shezmu knew they were coming .

He had them tied up with metal rods an a wall.

Seth finally woke up to find he was captured.

" They are here ! " Shezmu smiled as it was show time.

The great Ennead came charging in.

" Bastet it looks like you have been doing some recruiting," Shezmu laughed.

" Ash and Lucia are you kidding me !

You made them gods ? " Shezmu couldn't believe it.

" You better believe, this is for me and everyone you have heart and especially for Khnum. " Bastet cried out as Shezmu revealed her parents and Seth.

" I hope you have enough lives to save everyone here ? " Shezmu asked as she grabbed Ra throwing him to the ground as Sophie screamed and Connor held her back.

" You did this to me and the rest of us, you think he loved us ?

He didn't !

we were just weapons in his arsenal and I was made to be his executioner in case any of you rebelled or went against him.

That's why he must die first," Shezmu explained as he made his Ankh appear and was about to kill Ra Bastet stopped him and commanded his Ankh to him.

" Your right he made you and now his power runs through me," Bastet grabbed hold of Shezmu's Ankh and it was rusty and bloody and Bastet cleansed it of all the evil that Shezmu it in.

It returned to it's golden state.

" It's over for you," Bastet whispered as Khepri freed Seth and with the entire Ennead together Seth's wounds from Shezmu healed.

They were stronger.

" I Bastet goddess of Creation and protection I banish you ."

" I Seth god of the Desert storms banish you."

" I Ash lord of the Earth banish you,"

" I Sobek the god of rebirth banish you."

" I Thoth the god of wisdom banish you "

" I Lucia the goddess of love banish you ."

" I Khepri the lord of the air banish you "

" I Ma'at goddess of order and justice banish you forever." The Ennead had Shezmu surrounded as they banished him from space and time and existence.

He gave a final death cry. A scream full of pain unlike anything as he burnt and exploded with no remains.

" I could get used to this," Ma'at spoke.

" What about your work in the after life and underworld? " Thoth asked.

" Am literally there as we speak ! " Ma'at answered as Thoth loved the new recruit.

" What do you think of this life ? " Ash asked Lucia.

" Incredible," Lucia answered holding her ankh as Bastet went to help her father and mother and Seth helped Ra.

" You stopped him! " Connor was speechless as he hugged his daughter.

" Lucia ! " Sophie was happy to her again.

" You resurrected the Ennead am so proud of you," Ra said to Bastet.

" Not yet," she answered holding Shezmu's Ankh.

" This is the power of a god that can kill us and can manipulate memories and thoughts," Bastet explained to Ra.

" Don't tell me you are afraid of that,

I wasn't afraid when the prophecy spoke of one who would be my successor and will destroy Apophis and when it was going to be you.

I didn't fear you but I embraced you," Ra said to Bastet.

"So what should I do ?" she asked Ra.

"You choose better than I did and sometimes even for us gods it's humbling for us to know that we can also die cause every begining has an end and every end has its begining." Ra revealed to Bastet who hugged him when she saw Seth and she went to him.

"So what's next ?" Bastet asked as Seth pulled her in for a passionate kiss.

"I've waited centuries to do this," Seth whispered face to face with Bastet's .

"Then why did you stop ?" She whispered back as he smiled and proceeded to kiss her.

"We are going to heal "

"We are going to start again, together as one and unleash our power on the earth and make them believe,

Believe in us again," Bastet spoke to the Ennead as a new day was rising.

Nine Years Later.

"So much has changed," Bastet stood at the Ennead pyramid in the Aaru.

"You are the catalyst for all this change and if it wasn't for you we wouldn't be where we are today," Seth tells Bastet as they were ready for the wedding.

So much change had happened over the last nine years.

The Ennead was restored.

Everyone was happy to see Lucia alive and well again and now a god especially Emmy who was most affected by her loss.

Emmy over the next years she devoted herself and life to being a leader helping the next generation of Sha and Lynx come to be.

Embracing herself and her power as a Sha.

Ash and Ryan Ustet started a relationship and Ash got more confident and embraced his new role as a god.

Lucia decided to not reveal herself to her parents and decided to start a new better life as the goddess of love.

Connor finally got to know his daughter Bastet and her brothers got to know her well and they bonded.

Omar and Cairo basically teenagers now.

Sophie and Ra became a couple and Ra helped Sophie change her model agency to a place where inner beauty and self love was promoted and they called it the Maya Model Agency.

To Sophie Bastet was still her daughter and she was still Maya to her.

Bastet walked into the wedding ceremony and during the ceremony she couldn't help but think of the Ennead.

Everything she loved was on Earth and with Apophis gone they had no reason to stay in the Aaru holding him back.

It was time for change.

The wedding reception started and it was time for a speech and Bastet was asked to give it.

"What should I say," Bastet looked around.

"Besides I see beautiful faces all around, a family and best of friends.

Two sets of parents and the man I love,

I am glad I got a second chance at life to live again,

Am grateful for all you, it's why I've decided to change the rules for the Ennead.

We don't have to stay in the Aaru we are free to live with the mortals and walk side by side with them and love alongside them.

" Bastet said to them many of them couldn't believe it as Sophie got up running to hug Bastet.

Ryan and Ash finally could be together longer than before and build a life together.

Days later.

The Ennead was thought to be dead and some thought they would never be whole again.

Bastet decided to stay in Egypt for a while longer as she walked through the desert and saw the shadow of a jackal following her as she smiled.

" Seth I know it's you," She laughed as he showed himself and hugged her giving her the most passionate kiss before they both noticed the sun was rising and the other gods showing up from a far.

" It's time," Bastet smiled as she welcomed the newest member to the Ennead.

A fitting new worthy successor to the mantle of the god of death and nothing like Shezmu.

Bastet raised her hand and the other Ennead did the same as they all formed a circle as the sun was rising marking a new day.

All their Ankhs appeared in their hands.

" we have so much power together! " Lucia whispered.

" What will we do with it ? " Thoth asked.

" We can do anything! " Ash replied.

" What do we do Bastet! " Seth asked her as she smiled and her eyes changed.

" We will reshape the world, one that's better for everyone," Bastet smirked as their work had just only began.